I0742518

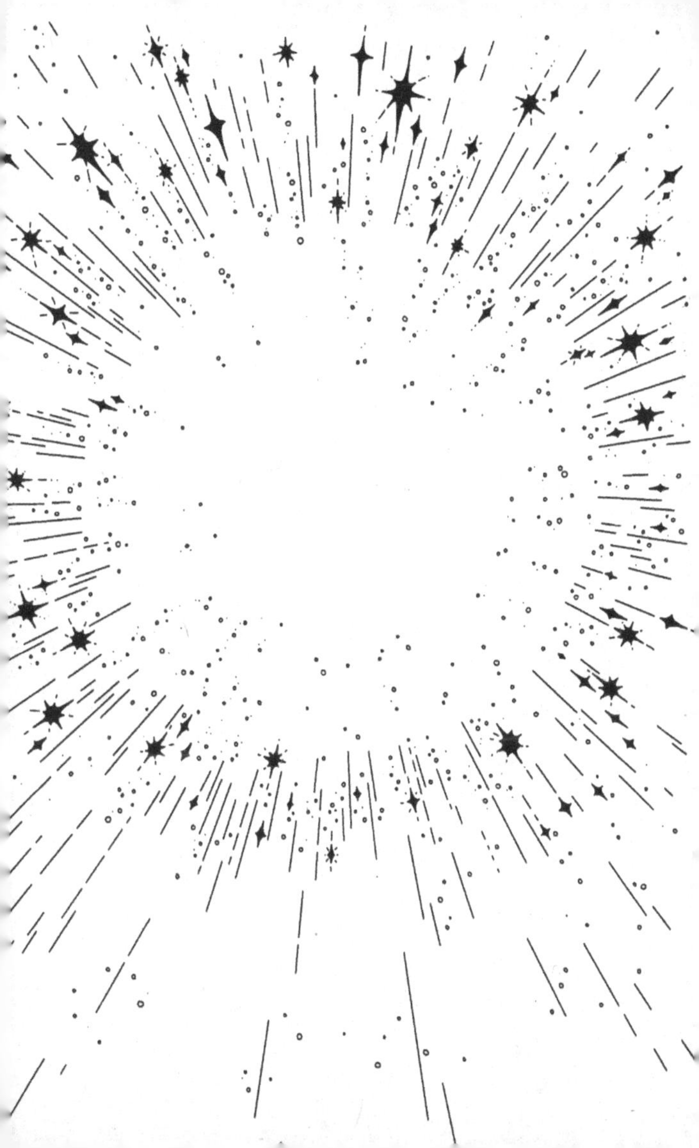

FORTHWRITES.COM

Songs of the Amaranthine, Pocket Editions
Book 1

Marked by Stars
Copyright © 2018, 2021, 2026 by FORTHRIGHT
A Song for Moon
Copyright © 2026 by FORTHRIGHT

ISBN: 978-1-63123-097-4

Illustrations: Mart Lett
Lettering: Asha-Loy de Souza
Jacket Design: Bumblebess
Editing: Wendy "LadyIsmene" Davis

TWINKLE PRESS

because your trust is precious to me

Embroidery proved an excellent medium for sigilcraft.

*"You shine. Like Soriel of the Dawning,
like Auriel of the Golden Seed.
Like every tale of the Kindred,
the Broken, and the Blessed, you shine."*

TSUMIKO AND THE ENSLAVED FOX

Marked
by
Stars

LOOR

Loor-ket's head turned as a chorus of howls welcomed another caravan, sending their skittish Kith sidestepping into a snowbank. Red-caped Amaranthine quickly moved among the reindeer, patting and soothing their kindred, no doubt reminding them that the Highwind pack did not consider them prey.

Once a decade, a migration heralded this festival week. The Song Circle guaranteed peace to all who made the journey. Here, in the depths of winter, the clans would fill the longest nights with light and life and laughter.

Representatives from every clan on the continent had been arriving for days, each bringing their share of peddlers, artisans, musicians, and storytellers. To *this* place. Grounds set apart since long ago, watched over by trees that were older than the oldest of them, kept safe by the Highwind wolves.

Staying well out of the way of the incoming

droves, Loor-ket slouched against the base of one of the Song Circle's sentinel pines. In summer, this vast meadow was all soft grasses and shy flowers, but Loor liked it best in winter, when hushing snows turned the circle into an echo of the moon—round, pale, and serene.

Not that there would be any peace for a while.

Dozens of lanterns ringed the expanse, one for each family unit, be it den or warren, flock or herd. By the opening song, there would be hundreds.

One of Loor's aunts directed newcomers toward the patchwork of tents arrayed among the trees. Someone was cooking with a spice that made his mouth water. A cheer went up from the direction of the bear camp. A wrestling match, no doubt.

From a nearby brush pile—reserve fuel for one of the many upcoming bonfires—a youngster from one of the squirrel clans tumbled into the open, checking the stride of the wolf coming Loor's way.

The wolf—who had the advantage of

being in his speaking form—scooped up the startled squirrel. No bigger than a wolf cub, the kit tucked neatly into the crook of the wolf's arm. But the youngster protested the cuddling. Sharp scolding and tail puffing ineffective, he transformed into a squirming boy with a thatch of red hair.

Too many other voices filled the meadow for Loor to catch any words—teasing on the wolf's part, grumbling on the squirrel's. With a tweak to the boy's pointed ear, the scamp was loose, running off to rejoin his friends. Pausing long enough to make sure the child found his way, the wolf resumed his slow trek toward Loor's vantage.

Like all Highwind wolves, he was tall and broad through the shoulders, with auburn hair and ghostly ice-gray eyes. But Beloor-dex hadn't yet attained the powerful musculature that would come with greater maturity. By right and by rite, he was counted as an adult, but he was still young.

They both were.

"You missed the ceremony." Beloor-dex slid down beside Loor and pressed close, matching his posture so they were hip-to-hip, knee-to-knee, ankle-to-ankle.

"No one noticed." Loor insinuated an arm around his brother's waist.

Beloor gently contradicted, "I did."

Loor offered his most disgruntled of grunts.

His brother's expression took on the added softness of sympathy.

Unbending a little, Loor kissed his twin's cheek.

Beloor-dex and Loor-ket were alike in every way except significance. Loor had missed his only chance to stand out by being born five minutes too late. Beloor was the Highwind pack's second tithe, born twentieth. His birthright set him apart from their whole family, including his younger twin. Which left Loor-ket lost in the middle of an ever-increasing pack.

At least he had Beloor. Their bond was enough. It had to be.

Loor sighed. "Well, what did they pick?"

"Elderbough and Moontide."

Two brothers just ahead them in the lengthy Highwind registry were establishing their own dens. They'd each earned the accompanying privileges—a mate, a name, a crest.

Loor let his chin drop to his chest. "They're good names. They have a nice ring to them."

"They'll sing well," agreed Beloor. "Next time, it will be your turn."

"No."

"Can't bear to leave me?"

Loor could hear the teasing in his brother's tone, but he answered seriously. "I'd never leave you alone."

His twin was too still, too silent.

"Bel?"

"There has been some … talk."

Loor wanted to flee from this new tone in his brother's voice, but he tightened his hold.

"Nothing is *settled*," Beloor went on. "Father only thought to mention it to me earlier today. I hardly know what to think."

If not for the fragility in his brother's gaze, Loor might have exploded with impatience. Somehow, he confined himself to a ragged, "What's happened?"

"A … a suitor."

He shook his head, not following. All their older brothers were settled, and none of their younger ones had reached the appropriate age. "A suitor," Loor echoed. "Who's a suitor?"

"Someone from the Ambervelte pack."

Loor knew the clan, of course. The Highwinds had ties to all the northern dens. An older sister had been courted by an Ambervelte, and her strength had been added to their pack. And there had been additional intermingling among his many nieces, nephews, and cousins.

Beloor said, "We played together as cubs."

Loor glanced at the Song Circle, as if the children and their games could give him some clue to the tentative hope creeping into his brother's expression. Although twinned births were far less common now—a cause for concerned debate during the last dozen festivals—Amaranthine were prolific. "*Everyone* plays here, no matter their clan."

"She remembered me."

A female? Loor could only shake his head.

Taking a deeper breath than needed for such a small voice, Beloor put the matter plainly. "I have a suitor. Terloo-soh Ambervelte says she will have me and no other."

Loor could hear the wonder in his brother's tone. A tenth child never pursued a mate or established a den of their own, for they served the whole pack. But once in a great while, one was chosen. A female because she was beautiful. A male because he was beloved.

He needed to say something. Anything. But the only sound that made its way past the constriction in Loor's heart and throat was a thin whine.

Loor-ket couldn't remember how his twin managed to get him away from the Song Circle. Had they walked together into the wood? Or had Bel carried him? Loor didn't recognize the clearing spread before them, a sheltered basin of pristine snow, filled with the serenity he craved ... and the solitude he feared.

Taking him by the hand, Bel led him along the edge to a place where the ground split.

They dropped into the gully, springing from stone to stone as they followed its jagged course. Walls rose up on either side, and dark recesses began to appear. Bel turned, took both of Loor's hands and rose from the ground. A short flight. Halfway up the sheer rockface, a narrow ledge served as a threshold. Thick hangings draped the entrance to a cave.

"My den," Bel whispered.

"You had a den?" Loor's heart wrenched, for he'd thought they shared everything. He'd never wanted anything of his own.

"This territory belongs to the Highwind tributes, for hunting and for training." Beloor drew him deeper inside, to a mound of furs. "Only my mentor knows I have a den, for he bid me establish one. But even he does not know this place. I warded it myself."

"I can tell." Even though much of Bel's training was a mystery, he'd freely shared all he knew of sigilcraft. Loor's lessons may have come secondhand, but the weaving of power came easily. It was a useful little secret for someone who wanted to avoid notice. An ironic skill for someone who was already beneath it.

"No one will come. No one can hear." Beloor shed his fine tunic and stole Loor's before pulling back heavy furs and jostling him under. Sliding in beside him, he pulled his brother close. "It's only us."

Loor clung to his twin, who made soothing noises and stroked his hair. Treating him like a child. Reassurances flowed—touch and taste and tangling. Beloor accepted Loor's possessive posturing without complaint. Affection for aggression. Balm for bitterness. Love for love.

Hours passed, and Loor refused to loosen his hold. If he let go, Bel would leave him for another. Nothing should ever be allowed to come between them. Beloor was Loor's, and Loor was Beloor's. This was how it had always been. This is how it should always be.

Days may have passed. Beloor woke Loor from his doze with a nip and nuzzle.

Loor opened his eyes, his arms tightening reflexively.

"All right, Brother. I do understand." Beloor's palm smoothed along Loor's spine, settling at the base of his tail. Intimate territory. "If you ask it, I will refuse her."

Here it was. All he'd ever wanted. Loor had won. At a word, Bel would be his and his alone. His twin would give up everything that had been denied him because he'd been born five minutes too soon.

Loor gasped for air. The words were so hard to say, but he pushed them out between sobs. "I will not ask it."

Bel cradled Loor, who howled and wept for the lonesome years he must endure. And when no more tears would come, his twin surprised him by falling apart. Loor comforted him in turn, giving as freely as he'd received.

On it went. Pressed together under the weight of ticklish furs, they whispered and wrestled, teased and tugged. All their growling and grappling was probably childish, but they'd soon be leaving child-hood behind.

This was their goodbye.

DEX

When the twins finally emerged, colors whispered through a night sky, shifting currents that seemed to dance in time to the distant piping of flutes.

"Are you hungry?" Bel asked solicitously.

Loor smiled and shook his head. A meal wouldn't touch the hollow he needed to hide.

"We could hunt," his brother said.

He may as well have added, *one last time.* Finality hung in the air, dragging Loor back even as it propelled Beloor forward. Strange, to be able to tell that his twin's heart already beat for another. So he declined with all the grace he could muster. "Let's join the feast."

Bel flashed a grateful smile and moved away, toward the Song Circle. Loor followed with flagging steps as their pack's Kith mobbed Bel. The sentient wolves were in his care, and he belonged to them. Loor had never considered them rivals for his twin's affection, for they understood the strength of a brother-bond.

Loor had planned to pact with Bel. To share a lifetime, to live as one. He had thought to rescue his twin from solitude, only to be the one left behind.

He hung back further, watching the rest of the Highwind pack welcome Beloor-dex with tails in full swing and glasses high. Loor's own tail hung limp as he marked the Ambervelte she-wolf whose whole posture spoke of relief.

Bel only had eyes for her, and his expression was something Loor had never seen, would never inspire. He was hers now. Loor felt his existence dwindle. *What do you become when the only one who ever saw you looked away?*

Nobody noticed him leave. No one raised questions when he jogged away from the lights, the life, and the laughter. Loor trudged determinedly along a faint trail, too lost in his morose thoughts to care where it might lead. The whimper drew him up short.

A voice—childish, chiding—slipped into his mind and startled him. *"I won't let you take her! She's mine!"*

Loor had been about to tread upon two cubs huddled together in the snow, a whelp and a weanling. These Kith were hardly visible in the snow, for the soft puff of their baby fur was pure white. "What are you doing way out here?"

The young male bared his teeth. *"Mine!"*

He didn't want to deal with cubs, but he couldn't very well leave them. Precious is the cub to their pack, and these two were obviously beyond boundaries.

"I'm not after your packmate. Is she a sister?" Loor reached for the whimpering ball of fuzz.

Jaws snapped at his hand.

"Easy now. She needs warming." He caught the baby's scruff, and his concern doubled. She was so small, she couldn't be weaned. "She should be with her mother. Let's bring her back together."

To his surprise, the older one took speaking form. "No!" he snarled. "Marnoo is *mine!*"

"She's also cold, hungry, and beyond help if *you* are her only defense," Loor said mildly. He loosened the bindings around his midriff and settled the baby against his skin. Closing his fur vest around her, he offered his free hand to the furious boy. "Peace, whelp. Would you have me ignore her needs?"

The boy scooted closer and grudgingly met his palm. "Moon-kin Ambervelte."

Loor ran his thumb over the back of the boy's hand, which was covered in soft fur. "This is unusual. Are you manifesting it for warmth?"

"This is how I am."

"I've never seen someone with your features." Loor took the boy's chin, turning his face. "Where are your ears?"

A set of pointed ears slowly lifted above his snowy hair, angled in an attitude of embarrassment. Loor was tempted to unbundle the boy to see how much of his body retained the fur of his true form. He murmured, "Extraordinary."

"Me and Marnoo have the same mam, but different sires." The boy was blushing badly, for the implication wasn't flattering. He tugged at Loor's sleeve. "Because she's a dex."

Comprehension came with lashings of curiosity. "Our pack has no Kith-kin. This is a pleasure!"

Moon's eyes lost some of their wariness. "You know what I am?"

"My twin is a dex, so I know what it means better than most. Your mam must be strong if the Amberveltes asked her to improve the bloodlines of your Kith."

The boy's tail began a tentative sway. Was he really so surprised to be recognized and accepted? Perhaps the other children had teased him. Loor pulled the boy closer. "Help me warm Marnoo while we chat. Is her sire another Kith from your pack?"

"No." The boy leaned trustingly against his shoulder. "Marnoo's sire is mam's bondmate. Da's a dex, too, and he fosters all those born to his den."

Loor could see the sense in uniting two tributes. Both would understand their role and its needs. "So your sister was born in true form." It was an old custom, but not unheard of.

Moon nodded. "And she's mine. Da gave her to me."

"Are you a tenth child, then?"

"Halfway." His tone and smile were shy. "I'm my sire's tenth cub, but the Maker doesn't require a tenth from the Kith."

"But you'll foster Marnoo in the manner of tributes."

"Yes."

"Good lad." Loor mussed up Moon's hair and gave his ear a cautious scratch. "I should get you back. Your sister needs to suckle."

"A little longer? I came prepared."

The boy brought a bottle from an inner pocket. With careful deliberation, he soaked a twist of soft cloth in the warm liquid. A twitching nose poked into the open, for the hungry cub had caught the scent of her next meal. As Moon offered her the sop, Loor quickly cupped his hand under it, lest they lose a single drop.

Marnoo suckled greedily and growled when Moon took the cloth away to wet it. Loor chuckled. "Patience, little one."

The cub opened her eyes, which were the rich copper of a harvest moon. Nosing his palm, she licked it clean and whined for more.

"Here, Marnoo," her brother crooned. "I brought plenty."

Loor smiled at the boy's earnest devotion.

He was a little young to foster a child, being a child himself, but Ambervelte decisions weren't Highwind business. So Loor struck a balance, addressing the boy as he would an equal while encouraging him to nestle in. Moon was doing his best. The least Loor could do was lend his support.

By and by, the bottle was emptied. Loor settled the sated cub against his belly and coaxed Moon closer. For a little while, they simply listened to Marnoo's wuffling snores. The peace of a den shared by three with none.

"Why are you out here alone?" Loor asked.

Moon's ears twitched. "Because I was lonely."

"Isn't it strange to go off by yourself if you're lonesome?"

The boy curled against him. "When everyone is happy except me, it's sadder than sad."

Loor found himself nodding. "Better to be happy with two than alone in the crowd."

"Yes. Just like that." Moon leaned up and kissed Loor's chin. "Tell me a story?"

"All the best storytellers will be at the Song Circle."

"A little longer?" wheedled the boy.

He gave in, telling the story of two brothers. One embraced the life of a dex, becoming the favorite of every Kith and respected by the Kindred. The other was his grumpy younger twin, whose only weapon was a needle and whose only friend was a Kith-kin.

"You sew?" asked Moon.

"Nothing so humble," drawled Loor. "I embroider."

"Do males embroider?"

Only the truth, and only a little. "There are so many cubs in my father's den, I'm quite sure my mother mistook me for one of her daughters. What can I say? I have a knack."

Moon giggled. He gently traced the fanciful stitching on Loor's festival tunic—white upon midnight blue. "Did you make this?"

"I did. Am I not grand in my finery?"

Furry fingers reached and rested upon Loor's cheek, and Moon's voice came into his mind. *Do they tease you?*

"Worse. They never noticed."

Moon's voice took on a fragile note. *They tease me.*

"Then you must be strong, like your mam

and your da and your sire. Trust their voices first. And mine." Loor leaned into his touch. "You have a place and a purpose. Sing your song with all your might."

The boy sniffled and sighed. "Glad I listened, even though I had to walk so far."

"Hmm? What do you mean?"

"Almost didn't come," Moon mumbled sheepishly.

Loor's bafflement doubled. Had someone sent the poor boy into the woods on a fool's errand? He had half a mind to track down the prankster. "Who sent you here?"

"A star came down and showed the way."

What an imagination. "*You* are the one who should be telling stories."

Moon's smile had a dreamy quality. "Loor?"

"Hmm?"

"Am I really your only friend?"

"Without you and Marnoo, I'd be wretchedly alone." Loor kissed his forehead. "I'm glad our paths crossed, Moon-kin. You are my friend for life."

STAR

Loor carried the sleeping cubs back into livelier territory. An elder elk's voice rose and fell, adding drama to the old sagas, and a colony of songbirds warmed their voices with hot brews and honeyed ciders. Bears paced through the complex patterns of a walking dance, weaving their way around a newly bonded pair.

He didn't catch sight of any Highwinds, but then he was watching for the lighter browns and pure white pelts for which the Ambervelte pack was known. Passing a cluster of owls and gray squirrels, he caught a peevish thread about the Woodacre clan, who'd gone from bold to brazen after forming an alliance with wolves.

The cheek.

Loor saw no reason for the fuss, except perhaps jealousy. The cozy clans liked protectors, and there were none better than wolves. But the packs usually kept to themselves—unfettered and free.

Good for the Woodacres.

Cooperatives were becoming increasingly common, out of fear for rogues and for human raiding parties. Trackers now reported annually to the pack leaders about these newcomers—colonists, trappers, explorers. They felled trees and tilled fields far to the east. Most Amaranthine saw no cause for concern; humans were slow-moving and short-lived. So far, the consensus at each Song Circle remained the same—watch and see.

Amaranthine lived wherever their counterparts flourished, watching over the animals, akin yet apart. If territories and migration patterns changed to accommodate humanity, then their people would change with them.

Humans were far from this place. The Song Circle, at least, was safe.

Loor had no trouble finding the cubs' temporary den. A lean wolf clansman in Ambervelte colors hurried his way, flicking through apologies and gratitude before gasping out a greeting. "He was only just missed. I was about to search."

"Da," murmured Moon, his tail giving a sleepy twitch. "I made a friend."

The male met Loor's gaze as he gathered the boy to his heart. "Is that so?"

"Moon-kin is a tribute to your den, and Marnoo is fortunate to have such a devoted protector."

Their da leaned close and pressed his cheek to Loor's, murmuring thanks and blessings. And as he carried the cubs homeward, Loor could hear the gentleness in his tone. "Why did you leave the tent?"

"A star came down," said Moon.

"You saw a falling star?"

"He didn't fall. He flew."

Loor shook his head and turned away, moving automatically toward the Highwind camp. Moon and Marnoo had needed him, and perhaps he'd needed them, too. If not for the cubs, he probably would have run and kept running, an aimless rogue, ill-prepared for life without a pack.

Like Moon, he'd left because he didn't want

to be alone. What good could come of that?

"Much good."

Loor stopped and turned, trying to pinpoint the speaker. He didn't recognize the voice, nor were there any wolf Kith close by. "Who spoke, please?"

His question was ignored, but the voice returned, clarion-clear. *"I am waiting."*

Baffled, Loor asked, "Where?"

"Come, prepare for your journey."

Loor scented the air but found nothing unusual. Even so, he rushed toward the small tent he shared with Bel. The moment it came into view, he knew something was wrong. Light poured from every gap and seam as if the interior was aflame.

He reached for the flap with a trembling hand.

"Gather your things."

Gritting his teeth, Loor stepped inside, only to be blinded by the figure awaiting him. Squinting through his lashes, he tried to understand what he was seeing. Could this be the star Moon claimed to have seen?

"Who ...?"

"I am Soriel. I stand in the presence of Heaven's throne, and I speak for the One who made all things."

Not a star then. Loor sank to his knees as suspicion became certainty—*angel.*

Soriel blazed across his senses—too bright, too clean, too much. Like the hair-raising tales of humans with fury in their souls, this creature put Loor in fear of his life. He was suddenly attuned to his shortcomings, ashamed of his selfishness, aware of his own stench. Groveling wasn't enough. He wanted to bury himself like spoor. Face covered, tail tucked, he groaned.

Then hands were at his shoulders. *"Lift your head, Loor-ket Highwind."*

When he obeyed, the dazzle was gone, and he was kneeling face-to-face with an angel upon the furs that carpeted the tent. Wings rustled. Skin flashed. Eyes blazed. But Soriel's posture promised peace as he presented his palms.

Loor met them, wanting to see if he was real. "You know my name."

Soriel smiled. *"And now you know mine. Is this not common ground?"*

He could barely breathe, let alone argue, so Loor only shook his head.

"You accepted Moon-kin's personhood." That shining countenance leaned closer. *"You did not hesitate to call him friend."*

This was so confusing. Loor's voice caught and tripped over itself. "I don't understand."

The angel stood, hauling Loor up so that his feet no longer touched the ground. He dangled there, as limp as his tail, waiting to see what the angel intended. But Soriel simply set him on his feet, then bent to bestow a kiss upon his forehead.

"Fear not, son of the packs. I bring a message."

He was aghast. The Maker had a message for him?

Soriel studied his face and smiled. *"Slave of the moon, lift your gaze to a place between. Shed your wildness to walk as men do, and in their midst, find a haven, forge a bond, found a future."*

Loor's skin prickled, and a shiver ran down his spine. "How do I do all that?"

"Go to the place I will show you. Follow my star. It will go before you." Soriel sketched a

scant tenth of the night's turning. *"Gather what you will carry and walk away. Do not run or leap or fly. Walk."*

Finally, Loor dared to ask, "Why?"

"Because every step demands your trust, confirms your choice, requires your patience. That is your pace." Soriel lifted shining wings and pointed to the east. *"There is your path."*

PATH

Before Loor had run across the cubs, he'd already committed to a course, no matter the consequences. He'd run away. He'd live alone. Unwanted, unneeded, he'd obeyed the impulse to disappear, sure that no one would miss him, even while hoping his brother would suffer a little for his sake.

A petty vengeance.

A pitiful reason.

Yet Loor would have run and kept running, an aimless rogue harboring bitterness. Feeling betrayed, he'd been ready to betray. To go without a word. To cut the only one who'd ever cared. But Moon and Marnoo had gotten in the way, forced him to pause, and given him time to rethink his recklessness. With cubs to carry, it was easier to admit that pack was precious.

In returning them to the Song Circle, Loor had remembered what it meant to hear the old stories, to have a voice in the song, to belong.

They had changed his course, and he'd known he would stay.

Only to be sent away. And without a word to the brother who might believe the worst and blame himself.

Bereft of Kith or Kindred. Estranged to the moon to which all wolves sang. Stripped of ties and—he'd been stricken to discover—his tail. Loor did wish that this mark of the Maker's favor hadn't cost him his pride as a wolf.

Loor rummaged in the small chest he shared with his brother, lifting aside embroidered sashes, uncovering boyhood treasures. His sewing kit and hunting knife were already in the carry-sack at his feet, but Loor wanted desperately to reassure his twin.

Bel's carving tools were no help, nor his brother's stash of wood, stone, and bone. Loor set them aside, but more items found their way into his pack—a medicinal pouch of herbs and ointments, three bowstrings, and an ember cache. He hesitated for a moment over a half-forgotten length of loomed cloth that had been one of his earliest assignments. It was clumsily made, but it was *his*, and it might prove useful.

Near the bottom, he found matching keepsake cords from his and Bel's whelping feast. They were a Highwind tradition, knotted with pledges of protection from both parents and packmates. Loor broke the bands to steal the anchoring bead from each. With no time to braid anything new, he pulled the cord from his topknot. Auburn hair hung loose around his shoulders, framing his face, hiding his expression as he threaded the twin stones, holding them in place with knots of unity, loyalty, and journeying.

"Please understand," he whispered.

Pressing his lips to the refashioned cord, he set it atop Beloor's neat stack of sleeping furs and fussed with its arrangement for the scant minute that remained between obedience and rebellion. Then he ducked under the drape that blanketed the entrance to the only home he'd known for more than a century and strode into an uncertain future.

Loor pulled the hood of his travel cloak up around his ears and skirted the Song Circle. To avoid notice, he'd hidden his pack beneath its fur-lined folds, but he attracted neither interest nor concern as he knelt beside a flagging cookfire to tease a few embers into the warded carrier that he knotted to one ankle.

Perhaps Soriel had rendered him invisible.

The alternative left him sad, yet surly.

Even though he wanted to run, run, run from the sting of his own insignificance, he heeded the angel's command and walked through the pain. Every step a choice.

Along an eastbound trail, he strode past a flock of jugglers, festive in their feathered waistcoats. Past steaming basins of sweet cider and mulled wine. Past a double-ring of dancers, lithe and lovely as they threaded through a naming dance for the new daughter added to their cloister. Past high-stepping maidens in the mossy drape of the Daphollow herd.

His sense of loss was vexing. Could he lose something he'd never possessed?

On and on he walked until the Circle's song

was nothing but memory, and the only voices were in his head.

Beloor saying, "Can't bear to leave me?"

Moon-kin saying, "A star came down and showed the way."

And Soriel saying, "Walk away."

DEN

Loor marked the new star in the sky and knew it for his guide. The twinkling blaze never moved faster than he could follow, and when his steps lagged to a standstill, the star sank from the heights and settled into a nearby tree like a bird come to roost. Which brought to mind old tales about sky imps and star clans, but Loor couldn't test his theories without breaking his pace to give chase. All he could do was watch and wonder and walk on.

After the passing of many days, his progress slowed, for the way grew difficult. Trees banished his view of the sky, and he was forced to trudge up and down hills that would have been nothing if only he could take to the sky. Yet here he was, scrabbling over every rock and rise.

He bound his feet and resigned himself to long stretches of uncertainty.

From time to time, the trees thinned, and he

glimpsed the distant shine of his star, which drew him onward, correcting his course through the long winter nights.

During brief hours of daylight, Loor hunted or slept. In the foothills of a mountain, he found a deep pool of dark water warmed by buried heat and stopped to bathe and rebind his bruised feet. In the process, he caught a glimpse of his reflection. He stilled, waiting for the ripples to settle and the surface to yield a startling truth.

Loor slowly lifted his hand to touch his forehead.

There, in its very center, gleamed a copper star.

The star stopped and stayed over a human village tucked into that same mountain's heights. On the third night, without any further sign of moving on, Loor had to concede that *this* was his destination, even though he couldn't fathom *why*.

Soriel didn't return with further instructions.

His star remained steadfast, confirming his arrival.

And so Loor began to explore the mountain valley and the mismatched pack of humanity that tended flocks and toiled in fields. This was his first encounter with people of this sort, and he kept his distance from their strange voices, labors, and smells.

One season passed into another, and the busyness of the humans left Loor even lonelier than before. They talked and laughed. They formed little packs and cared for young. They tamed animals and used them for meat and for milk and even for companionship. He was most curious about the tame canines that came to heel for hunters and herders alike.

Dogs.

While similar to wolves, their features varied in interesting ways. Some he found quite ugly, but there were beauties in their midst. They had no words, being dumb beasts, but their barks and body language reminded him of home and stoked a craving for the closeness of one's packmates.

Curiosity carried him closer to their strange

dens, only to set off a chorus of warning barks. He admired their protective instincts but chafed at their exclusion. Which is what drove him to take his truest form.

On all fours, he was a little larger than a wolf. Nose to the ground, he savored the scents that were growing more familiar. The trapper and his sled dogs. The shepherd and his herders. The headman and his kennel of hunting dogs.

The latter drew him unerringly to the man's barn. Loor transformed long enough to let himself inside, then reverted to the form of a ruddy wolf with silver eyes. Only one dog had been closed in for the night, a bitch and her litter. He approached with care, and she seemed to understand that he was something other than a threat.

Instinct worked in his favor.

She recognized him as a protector, and after long weeks alone, he was able to enjoy the scents and sounds of a proper den. Her pups tumbled around him, and she looked on with tail slowly wagging. Nightly, he returned, and always he found welcome.

And in finding this scrap of peace, he threw himself into his newfound role.

He let himself go, following instinct, abandoning words. This was his den, his territory, so he prowled the headman's borders, protecting his holdings. But Loor's peaceful days ended far too soon, for a dog's life was short.

When the bitch breathed her last, he roved the village, seeking a new den. What he found changed everything.

A farmer with vast herds on the high slopes north of the village had purchased a new bitch—a leggy hound with intelligence in her gaze. He kept her shut away because she was in heat, and Loor liked her looks and the privacy her owner had so thoughtfully provided.

There was a brief outcry when the farmer realized that his best hunting dog was pregnant, but no one in his household knew where to lay blame. Perhaps the pups would give some clue to their father's identity.

Unconcerned by the circulating speculations, Loor took to patrolling this farmer's boundaries. He protected the man's herd, his crops, and even warned off a dray of squirrel Kith. Before the week was out, he'd been spotted by more than one villager, and tales of a red wolf with ghostly eyes began to spread.

Loor watched over the bitch and waited, and this waiting was not the same as waiting on stars. For these were days he knew how to number, and their end would bring a new life into the world. This hound carried his cubs. No, she was no wolf. Her young would be pups. *His* pups.

NAME

The weight of *that* realization drove Loor into speaking form for the first time in years. He shuddered to think what might happen to the pups if they bore any resemblance to the dreaded red wolf. Before their birth, he needed to find a better den for his pack.

Sitting cross-legged in the straw, he waited to see if the expectant mother would recognize him in speaking form. Loor extended a hand, and said, "Forgive me for not offering my pledge until now, dear one. I am with you and will keep you. Can you accept an ill-mannered mate?"

She licked his fingertips and scooted forward to lay her head upon his knee.

"You deserve a name." He gazed thoughtfully into her eyes, and at length, he said, "I'll call you Generous, since your gifts are good. I will treasure them."

The only answer he received was the wag of her tail.

"I'll find a good place," he promised.

That night, he searched the sky and found his star, burning faithfully over the village's center. He could not leave, and so he looked for a den within its boundaries. Up and down the beaten tracks, he considered his options, which were few. In the end, he chose a disused animal barn at the edge of a fallow field belonging to the headman. Snug against an embankment, it would be spared the worst of winter's winds, and it wasn't readily visible from any road. With careful warding, the village would soon forget it ever existed.

Generous only carried one pup, and she carried the little one well past the usual season for birthing. More waiting. At least now, Loor could fill the hours. He reinforced the shed, shoring up its foundations and digging into its dirt floor. Adding a fire pit took days, and he spent weeks filling the loft with fragrant branches and harvesting grasses for bedding.

Loor's first wards had been hastily drawn in the dirt, but he needed something that would withstand the curiosity of critters and the whims of weather. He couldn't pull anything complex out of midair, so he needed an anchor—wood, stone, paper. Crystals were ideal, but scarce. Inspiration struck, and he sifted through the meager contents of his pack, coming up with his neglected sewing kit.

Working sigils into fabric couldn't be any more complicated than stitching a crest. He was on his third attempt at anchoring wards into embroidery when Generous finally showed signs of delivering her pup.

His son.

Loor named him Path, because every step of his journey had brought him to this place. He spent hours curled around the pup, whose baby fuzz was decidedly red. "Will you favor your sire?" he crooned, tugging at one tiny drooping ear.

Path's answering whine was not a sound, but a thought.

Loor's hand shook, and his eyes misted. "Do you have a voice, Path?"

Within days, there was no doubt, for the pup's burbling and babbling was a constant in Loor's mind. He was a Kith-sire. He was no longer alone.

Embroidery proved an excellent medium for sigilcraft, especially when Loor twined his own hair with the threads. While not as potent as the illusions of the trickster clans, he was able to deflect notice and deter pests. As Path grew, Loor expanded his holdings to include the entire pasture. Room to romp and tussle and laze in the sun.

Generous bore him a second son, and Loor called the pup Soon, because he still chose to believe that Soriel's promise would find its fulfillment.

Her last pup, another male, he called Trio, because now there were three voices in Loor's head, and his loneliness was at a low ebb.

Was this part of the Maker's purpose, setting him apart from his pack in order to live as a dex? While Loor hadn't been born twentieth, he'd shared an equal place in his mother's twentieth pregnancy. Where the Highwind pack had quibbled and divided, perhaps the Maker was asserting a prior claim. It was a comforting thought.

This mountain, this village, this den—he knew they must be his, for his star never strayed. But even knowing he was in the right place, Loor grew restless. Ranging through the human community, he searched for a way to add to his pack.

Finding a young sled dog with eyes the color of a winter sky, he took her for his own. He called her Restless.

She gave birth to another Kith, a son he named Pace, to remind himself that the seasons were not his to direct. And before her brief life ended, she bore a second pup. This son he named Rile, because a piece of his soul howled against Heaven.

Thus far, all his sons resembled their sire, with shaggy red-brown fur. The variances they inherited from their mothers. Generous' pups had drooping ears, and Path had inherited the lively brown eyes Loor had found so lovely.

Restless' pups were stockier, with curling tails and blue eyes.

He took them on hunts, taught them the woodland trails, and showed them the heavenly star that blazed above their home. They ranged over the whole of the mountain, which he urged them to protect—both it and its human community. And the villagers added to their store of tales. His pack had become the Demon Dogs of Denholm.

A newcomer to the mountain brought a new breed of dogs. Loor quietly absconded with a pup, who quickly grew into a gentle-natured companion. Beauty had a lavish coat of golden hair, which he never tired of brushing, and in due course, he needed that same comb to keep his first daughter's red-gold fur in order.

She became Dawn, because this was a new beginning.

His Kith were the first Amaranthine dogs, and he took the name "First of Dogs." His children never learned the name Loor-ket Highwind, nor did he hand down any wolf lore. When he sang, it was of the descent of an angel and the rise of a star.

Though they had no crest, and their den was little more than a shed, they were a clan unto themselves. He took the name Starmark, and his children knew him as Glint.

BOY

Why do you keep taking mates?"

Glint turned to face his eldest son. "What kind of question is that?"

"Your mate is barely cold, and your eye is already wandering over the village bitches. Does full blood run hotter than half? Or are you just a greedy rutter?"

There was a bitter edge to Path's voice, and Glint could feel the depths of his disdain. But he couldn't bring himself to be upset with his son. "Is that what you think of me?"

Path's tail tucked. *"Sometimes."*

He grabbed his son by his considerable ruff, hauling until the dog's bowed head butted into his breastbone, making it easier to lavish affection on his four-footed child. Path and his siblings were tall as moose and burly as bears, but little more than pups in the eyes of their sire.

"I take no pleasure in watching a mate's life wink out after so brief a bonding," said Glint.

"Have you ever seen me handle a bitch in an unworthy manner?"

The answer came soft and earnest. *"Never."*

Glint had taken many mates over the decades, and most had borne him a pup or two. "Your mothers have each been dear to me." Glint searched for a way to explain his choices. "Their deaths do break my heart, but I've resolved to endure the losses. These bitches are both your heritage and our future."

Path grumbled, *"You want more pups."*

"Naturally."

"Why?"

"For your sake. For the sake of our pack." Glint asked, "Would you banish any of your younger brothers or sisters from this world? Would you deny Trio his newfound bond with Dawn? Would you turn down the chance at an equal match, should one of your half-sisters or future nieces welcome your pursuit?"

"I don't want a mate."

"Why not?"

"I have you." More softly, *"That's enough ... for me."*

"Path." Glint threaded his fingers through

shaggy fur. "Please don't think I added to our pack because I found my firstborn lacking."

His son whined and nosed the shining star left behind by an angel's kiss.

Glint rested his forehead against Path's. "I came to this mountain alone, but your birth ended my solitude. Your steadfastness has been my support, and your happiness is my only wish."

"*We are not the same.*" Path's voice turned stern. "*Stop asking me to find your version of happiness, when I have chosen my own.*"

"When did my son learn wisdom?"

Taking the question literally, Path earnestly answered, "*A little at a time. Mostly on clear nights, when a soft wind blows from the east.*"

Glint chuckled. "And why are *those* considered favorable conditions?"

Path's tail wagged. "*They are the only times you can hear our star singing.*"

Weeks passed before the winds took a

favorable turn. Gentle gusts carried a piercingly sweet song Glint hadn't even realized he should be listening for. For two centuries and more, the star had kept its distance from him, but its lyric promised that hope was near. And drawing nearer.

Dawn's first litter arrived in springtime, two females—Hope and Help—and a scrappy male he called Romp.

Glint had wondered why the domesticated dogs he'd claimed only ever bore one pup at a time. Highwind Kith often had litters of three or four wolf cubs. Dawn's litter meant that their pack could transition from addition to multiplication.

If only he could bring in a few Kith from other packs. Would wolves willingly mingle with his sons? Or would that mean losing their distinction as dogs?

He was muddling through different approaches to the problem when the shed door opened with a violent *creak*. Since he and his children generally made use of a convenient gap in the back wall, those hinges hadn't budged in more than a century. And there on the threshold stood a human child.

Small and brown and barefoot, he had straight black hair hanging around his shoulders. His pants seemed to have been sewn from skins, but his shirt was the homespun typical of the humans in this village. But Glint guessed he wasn't one of the village brats. Any of them would have taken one look and run screaming. If not from him, then from Path, whose flank currently served as his backrest.

But this boy took a step forward, babbling in an unintelligible language.

Glint grunted. "You have a lot to say, but your language is strange. It's no use, boy. I can't respond in kind."

The boy pursed his lips in frustration, intelligence shining in black eyes. He came two steps further into the den and spoke again, slower. Tugging at his own ear, he gestured at Glint's. Pointed ears were one way in which humans could be distinguished from Amaranthine in speaking form.

To acknowledge their difference, Glint touched the tip of an ear. "Yes, boy. I'm different from you, and we both know it."

Again, the boy spoke, and this time, he enunciated each syllable. The word was strangely accented, but clear enough—Amaranthine.

"You know the word for me?" Glint chuckled and offered the *correct* pronunciation.

The boy muttered it under his breath a few times, practicing the syllables.

"What is he saying?" asked Path. *"What is that word?"*

"He knows what we are. This human child is somehow familiar with our race."

"We are Starmark."

"Starmark is our clan name. We are the first of the dog clans, but every creature has its Kindred, and all those clans together have one beginning, one Maker, one purpose, and one name. We are Amaranthine."

"Amaranthine," echoed the boy, his pronunciation correct.

Nodding, he tapped his chest. "Glint Starmark."

The boy shuffled closer, hands outstretched, tone questioning.

Glint gestured him forward. "It's your good fortune to be correct, but whoever taught you the form for greetings should be reprimanded for his accent."

The boy wriggled his toes and tried a different word.

"Peace," Glint said clearly. "Peace, little fool. My son and I mean you no harm."

Glint was rewarded with a gap-toothed grin, and the boy closed the distance with a skip in his step. Without a trace of concern for Glint's claws, he met palms.

"Brave little thing," remarked Glint.

"What do we call him?"

"Let's find out." Glint tapped his own shoulder and repeated his name. Then he tapped the boy's scrawny chest and arched his brows inquiringly.

The grin widened, and the boy mimicked Glint, tapping his own shoulder. "Waaseyaa." And without a trace of shyness, Waaseyaa reached up to touch Glint's thick hair.

He huffed and bowed his head, inviting the boy's curiosity.

Suddenly, fingers grazed his forehead.

Glint didn't move, but he lifted his gaze to find the boy's face inches from his. Excitement added a sparkle to his eyes, but his tone was entirely serious. "Glint Starmark," he said.

"Waaseyaa," he replied dutifully.

With a laugh, the boy threw his arms around Glint's neck and babbled nonsense, then kissed his cheek. The touch sent an unanticipated thrill through Glint's soul—dazzling in its brightness, fainter but familiar nonetheless.

Here was something he hadn't tasted in many long years. Not since an angel kissed his forehead.

PEACE

Path asked, *"Is this bad?"*

"It might be," Glint muttered. The boy had gone away, only to return leading a burly man with pale eyes, whose frizzled beard looked in need of a good brushing.

"I don't know his scent. Where did he come from?" Trio was understandably antsy with strangers so near his pups. *"How did he find us?"*

Soon asked, *"Did they break your wards?"*

"I'll check them later," promised Glint. "Calm your hackles. I think they're simply curious about us."

This new stranger was armed, but he never once reached for the weapons at his belt. And he listened more than he spoke. After Waaseyaa finished telling his side of a story that seemed unnecessarily long, the man nodded and turned to Glint with palms extended.

To Glint's surprise, the man addressed him in heavily-accented Amaranthine. "This village fears demon dogs."

Glint snorted. "My Kith and I aren't demons."

"I see. I know." The man grimaced apologetically. "This village is gone. Empty. This village is ours. We will stay."

Things had been quieter lately. But Glint's only thought had been for Dawn's litter. How much had he missed? He shook his head and firmly declared, "I'm staying."

With a sign for peace, the man said, "Good. Stay. Good. Welcome you. Welcome us?"

His Amaranthine was an old hinge, rusty from disuse. Glint chose simple words. "As long as you leave me and my pack in peace, you can do as you please."

The man gestured a helpless apology. His words were too few for much understanding.

Waaseyaa spoke again, waving between himself and Glint.

"Learn." The man indicated the boy and searched his vocabulary. "Learn. Speak. Teach?"

"You want me to teach the boy?" Glint considered Waaseyaa, whose hopeful gaze needed no translation. "He seems quick enough, and I can rid him of your wretched accent."

Another hesitant headshake.

Glint sighed and said, "Good. Teach Waaseyaa. Good. Peace."

Relief and happiness shifted into the humans' scents.

The man said, "Good. Glad. Grateful." With a wince, he added, "Too long ago Gerard learn. Mother-kin from enclave. Silverprong."

"That explains the accent." Glint chuckled and explained to his sons, "The deer clans speak with an adorable lisp."

"What's an enclave?" asked Path.

"I have no idea. Once the boy has the words, we can ask him." Glint stepped forward to cover the man's palms, carefully enunciating his name and going so far to introduce his Kith as well.

The man nodded to each in turn, then offered his own name. "Gerard Reaver."

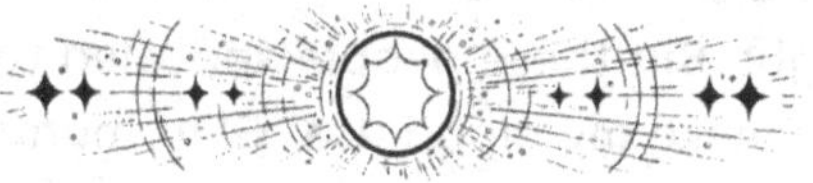

Glint searched for and found the gap in his wards and reinforced his boundary, etching some additional sigils into the dirt for good measure. While he was at it, he watched to see what his new neighbors were doing. The air hung thick with strange smoke and the stringent odors of bruised herbs. He recognized salt and wax and the tang of ore, but there was a musk he'd never encountered.

Reaver's men were a strange bunch. On the surface, they behaved as the previous villagers had—herding and tilling and making improvements to houses and barns. But they also razed three houses in order to expand the village center, and weeks of back-breaking labor went into the construction of a low stone wall that encircled all the occupied homes.

Most unusual was the way their presence appealed to him. With the former villagers, once he'd grown accustomed to their scents and noises, he hadn't given them much thought. But these people appealed to him. "They make my blood rise," Glint murmured. An unsettling thought occurred to him.

"They make me hungry."

To varying degrees, all of Reaver's men piqued his interest, but none more than Waaseyaa.

Path was the only one to voice similar inclinations. *"Would they taste good?"*

"I pledged peace," Glint reminded. "Would you make your father a liar?"

"I don't want to eat them. I want to understand why they steal into my thoughts." Path cocked his head to one side. *"Our boy is best. I want him near because I am gladder, lighter, stronger when he is near."*

Glint grunted, for Path's words echoed the feelings that had been growing in his own heart. "We used to guard the villagers. Now we must guard ourselves around them."

Path's tail beat the ground. *"Can we keep him?"*

"Waaseyaa?"

"He's the brightest. He's the best."

"We can't claim him without consent," said Glint. "But we have our own allure. He seems fascinated by our differences, our language, our customs."

"We should keep him."

Glint slipped his arm around Path's thick neck, leaning into his bulk. "While they live longer than a common dog, humans have short lives."

Path whined.

"I'll do my best to encourage his interest."

But wooing Waaseyaa was far from difficult. The boy was not only enamored of Glint and his pack, he was lonely. He lingered in their den after their lessons were done. Many evenings he stayed long after the humans' usual dinner hour, nestled between Path's forepaws, playing with Dawn's pups.

On such nights, Gerard came looking for him. "You should not impose!" he chided.

Glint hastily assured, "My den is brighter for his presence. He's welcome."

Conversation had grown easier with his eager young pupil. For every word Glint taught Waaseyaa, he was given its equivalent in exchange. Glint was learning Reaver's language, and the man offered gruff gratitude for the consideration.

"Can I stay?" wheedled Waaseyaa.

A dozen tails beat their bedding of summer

hay in unanimous approval.

Gerard tugged at his beard, his gaze slanting thoughtfully to Glint. "You are willing?"

He signaled affirmative. "The boy may consider my den his home, and I will consider him a packmate."

"I cannot say which of you has more courage." Gerard tousled Waaseyaa's hair, then gave him a push in Glint's direction. "But I do know that we are honored."

That night, Waaseyaa clambered into the midst of the pack, and Glint allowed his children and grandchildren to vie for the boy's attention. However, once Waaseyaa's eyes grew heavy, Glint asserted his right. Remaining in speaking form for once, he waded into the mound of fur to pull the drowsing boy against his side.

Waaseyaa stirred and blinked up at him, then smiled and nestled in.

Glint rumbled approval.

Long into the night, he basked in the boy's trust and wondered if this is what it would have been like if his children could take speaking form. Did Beloor nestle with sons and daughters in this way? Would he be more shocked to learn that his tailless brother had founded a clan of dogs or that his pack now included a human boy?

CREST

Glint hadn't slept so deeply since the night he and Bel had smuggled star wine into their den to toast their attainment. Jaws closed over his hip, and Path's voice was a shout in his mind.

"Please, wake! Wake up! Why can't you hear me, Da?"

He grunted and reached for the offending muzzle. "Calm down. I'm awake."

Path whined.

"I'm awake," Glint repeated, though he felt loose and languid. He started to sit up, only to recall the boy currently using his shoulder for a pillow. Nothing else seemed out of place. In low tones, he asked, "What is it?"

"The star is singing."

Waaseyaa didn't notice when Glint eased from the pile to follow Path out into the night.

Urgency bade Glint to rush, but even now, years after the command was given, he couldn't bring himself to disobey. So he *walked* through the pasture, and he *walked* the narrow path that led to their property's high point. He resolutely checked his stride. Every step a choice.

And as he walked, he shed his strange stupor. The night was moon-bright and balmy, with a hint of distant rainstorms on the wind. Tonight's song carried well, and it lifted Glint's spirits. Here was a psalm of beginnings and of bonds, a tale of those between and of blessings. But a warning note shivered through every refrain, telling of a people touched by power and the dangers of their allure.

Glint stood his ground and listened until dawn took the sky, humming along until he was sure he would remember every word. Because if the song was right, then Reaver's people were a danger—not only to him, but to themselves. And Waaseyaa most of all.

"What are you doing?" Waaseyaa hung over Glint's shoulder. "Can I try?"

"You want to learn to sew?"

"I want to learn ... this." The boy's finger trailed along the edge of Glint's threadwork.

Glint had settled on a design for the Starmark crest, which included a sinking moon, half-hidden by the horizon. The ascending star matched the blaze on his forehead. But most important—and most time consuming—was the tracery of protective sigils around the border. Glint hoped to work the wards for a barrier directly into the cloth.

"Sigilcraft interests you?" he asked.

"A new word?"

"Two words in one—*sigil* and *craft*." Touching the circular design, Glint said, "This is a sigil. I am its crafter. I make them."

Waaseyaa continued to brush the edge, as if testing a boundary. "What is it for?"

"It will protect you. It will protect me." He held up his hand. "Like a wall."

The boy gasped. "You are a ward?"

"I am Glint."

"Our wards are not here yet, but when they come, they will bring the stone wall to life." He fumbled for a moment, then switched to his own language. "A barrier."

"*When they come?* Who is coming ... more like Reaver?"

"Many more. And Amaranthine." Waaseyaa's hands described circles in the air. "We cleared the center, and we're building the wall. The rest are coming, and they will share Wardenclave with us—Fullstash and Dimityblest and Duntuffet."

Glint recognized those clan names—squirrel, moth, and rabbit. "What is Wardenclave?"

"Two words in one." Waaseyaa leaned forward, eager to share this heretofore unmentioned bit of news. "*Ward* and *enclave*. We must build a barrier."

"What are you keeping out?"

Waaseyaa's eyes lost their shine. "Everywhere we go, they follow. We are hunted. We are prey." He hesitated, then quietly added, "They took my family."

Responding to the fear and sadness in Waaseyaa's scent, Glint set aside his needlework and tugged him onto his lap. "I didn't know there was anything that hunted humans."

"Amaranthine."

Glint was almost afraid to ask. "Why would Amaranthine hunt humans?"

"To eat." He looked up into Glint's face. "They want our souls."

With the warnings of his star reeling through his mind, he shook his head incredulously. "If Amaranthine predators are your enemies, why weren't you afraid of me?"

Waaseyaa hesitated.

Glint waited.

Finally, the boy admitted, "Because you only looked surprised."

"Anyone would be, when a strange child strolls past several decades worth of sigilcraft." He picked up his handiwork again and scrutinized the delicate balance of its seal. It should work. It would have to. "Give me your shirt."

With no real need for sleep but an abundant need for clarity, Glint took his stitching outside. Away from Waaseyaa, he was more himself, but having been with the boy, his stitches were more potent, and his sigils shimmered with strength he hadn't known he possessed.

Path's description from those earliest days was proving true and truer. Glint whispered, "Gladder. Lighter. Stronger."

By moonlight, he duplicated his crest, embroidering it directly onto Waaseyaa's shirt. It was as much a claim as it was a promise of protection. The boy was his now. A fosterling.

Mid-high saw the task finished, so Glint called the Kith into a circle, to bear witness to the boy's attainment. "Take your shirt back. Wear it well."

Waaseyaa quickly obeyed, pulling the cloth away from his skin to admire Glint's addition. "A sigil for me?"

"That's the mark of my clan, the Starmark crest. Wearing it means you belong to our den." He dropped to one knee and looked him in the eye. "We are your pack."

"What kind of pack?"

Glint grinned. "We are dogs."

"Den is like ... *house*?"

"More than a house, not just a building."

Glint offered him new words. "Home. Pack. *Mine.*"

"I belong to Glint?"

"Do you have a family name? What is your clan called?"

The boy blinked. "Reaver found us and saved us and took us in. He shared his name and keeps us safe until the enclave is ready. I was his, but he gave me to you." Touching the crest on his shirt, he asked, "What should I be called?"

Glint considered birthnames of great importance, so he pressed. "How did your mother call you?"

"Waaseyaa means 'first light from the rising sun.'" He shook his head. "I was born among the trees, but I have no roots. I escaped. I ran. I wander."

Once he learned more words, Glint would talk to Gerard. To one made for dens, endless wandering sounded wretched. He wanted to know the bounds of his territory and to learn its every whiff and way. To protect it and to find pleasure in its peace. And to share it.

"You are a Reaver, then?" Glint asked. "Or

would you like to be called Starmark?"

"Both are good names," Waaseyaa said tentatively. "But I will have a new name when … when I keep my promise. I should wait."

The boy's scent twisted with secrets and fears, and Glint pulled him close. "You do not share my name, but you bear my crest, Waaseyaa the Wanderer. If you have made a promise, then you must keep it, and I will be your support."

He clung and mumbled, "I can still belong to Glint?"

"Never doubt that, boy."

Glint was pleased to see that his sigilcraft worked well enough. Waaseyaa's presence was snug as a nutmeat in its shell. The giddying soul no longer stoked his senses and stirred his appetite. Even better, he was well-hidden from the predators who might still be on the hunt. But with Waaseyaa muffled, it was possible to pick out other points of brightness throughout the village.

Reaver's men might be a raggle-taggle crew of mismatched humanity, but they gathered at the same circle. Those who worked on the wall, those who cleared the village center, those who minded the flocks, those who scavenged in forest and field—Glint could sense them all.

And that meant they were in danger.

PACT

When Swift, the white-muzzled bitch who'd borne him both a daughter and a son, succumbed to her years, Glint did not seek a new mate.

Path noticed.

"The boy demands too much attention." Glint wasn't sure why he felt the need to make excuses. "You have to admit he's as bad as Dawn's litter for getting into things."

He had only ever had to deal with one pup at a time, so three left them feeling rather overrun.

"You will devote yourself to him?" asked Path. *"Is he your new mate?"*

Glint settled back, needing to explain. "There are different kinds of mates, but all require our loyalty. I took your mothers as mates to sire Kith, and so I am not alone. Denmates share a home. Packmates share blood. Pactmates share a promise. And if I were to choose and pursue an Amaranthine female, a mate who was my equal in every way, we would be bondmates."

Path's ears pricked and dipped, ending in cockeyed confusion. *"When you take a village bitch, it is for breeding without bonding?"*

"Your mother was Generous, and while she remained at my side, I pursued no other. But because she was a creature without words, my promise could not be returned. While I'd never say that made her devotion to me less real, we were unequal."

"Is Waaseyaa your equal?"

Glint pondered that and finally decided, "We are not the same, but we both have words. I cannot imagine treating him as less than I am, nor would I be tempted to revere him as more than I am. So yes, he is my equal."

"And me?"

"Are we not reasoning together?" He reached up and tugged his son's ear. "We are equal."

"Even though I cannot speak as you do?"

"You have words, and I can hear them. When I speak, you understand me. We are not the same, but what two individuals are?" Glint grinned up at his eldest. "We share the bonds of blood and of home."

"Packmates. Denmates."

"Yes."

Path asked, *"Would you share a pact with me?"*

Glint stood and wrapped his arms around his son's thick ruff. "If you yearn for more, I will not refuse. What promise shall we make?"

"I have watched you with Waaseyaa. You want a son."

"I have you. I have your brothers and sisters."

"Promise me you will find your equal. Promise me that your next mate can return your promise and become your bondmate." Path softly added, *"You deserve a true son."*

Glint growled. "You *are* my son. I'm proud of all of my children."

Path's head drooped, his ears low, tail tucking.

"Why would the son who so jealously guards his place at my side ask me to pursue another?" Glint was both angry and ashamed that his attentions to Waaseyaa had hurt his son. Path had been with him the longest, knew him best. It made no sense, and he grumbled, "Me, take a bondmate? And this from the stubborn whelp who refuses one."

Path whimpered.

"I'm not angry." Glint held on tight and stroked his son's fur. "I *am* confused, though. Who put this nonsense in your head?"

"Your star."

"I hadn't realized it was singing again."

"The boy demands much of your attention."

Glint did not appreciate having his excuses turned against him. He grunted and growled, but only asked, "Well?"

Path hesitated a moment. *"Do you have a brother?"*

"I have many, but they are far from this place."

"But ... a best-loved brother?"

He didn't want to speak of the past, but neither could he deny it. "The star has been singing about me?"

Path nodded—a human quirk he'd learned from Waaseyaa.

Glint heaved a sigh. "My twin. I loved him better than any other person in this world. But he was chosen by another, and he liked her pursuit."

"Pursuit?"

"Like when Dawn came into her own, and

Soon and Rile noticed, but she showed her preference for Trio." He looked away. "I made the same promise to my brother that you made to me—to be his and no one else's. But a female who was his equal made an offer for him. He was her choice, and she became his choice."

Path was silent for a long time. *"Females choose?"*

Glint chuckled. "In a bond between equals, each chooses the other. But in Bel's case, the female chose first. It's hard to explain. He was a dex, so that's the way it had to be."

"Are you a dex?"

"I live as one."

Path's tail took on a sway. *"I understand. Now will you share my pact?"*

"In a pact of this nature, promises are usually exchanged." Inspiration hit. "How about this? You want me to take a bondmate so you can meet my 'true son.' In return, you must take a bondmate someday, so that I can meet your son."

"I do not want a mate."

"If you are going to ask the impossible of

me, I should be able to ask as much of you."

"*Why impossible?*"

"Path, there are no Amaranthine dogs for me to pursue. I am the First of Dogs, and there are no others."

His son's eyes narrowed. "*You were born without a mother?*"

"My mother is a wolf."

One ear cocked. "*How does a wolf become a dog?*"

"By listening to stars." Glint's smile turned wry. "By walking away."

"*What about your son?*"

"Which son? I have many."

"*The son born to your bondmate.*"

"What if it's a daughter?" Glint asked, just to be contrary.

"*Would they be a Starmark?*" asked Path. "*Would they be a dog?*"

He allowed himself to imagine such a future. "Yes. A dog."

Path nosed his father's forehead, then licked his cheek. "*Be my pactmate.*"

"I don't want to make a promise I can't keep."

"*It will be kept.*" His son's voice had a teasing

lilt. *"Your star said the moon is tracking you, and its radiance will touch your face."*

"What's that supposed to mean?"

"You are chosen," Path said simply.

Glint didn't exactly doubt his son or the star. Both were his by the Maker's design. All he could do was wait and watch and wait some more. And work with Waaseyaa in the meantime. "Yes, Path. I accept your pledge and give mine in return—a son for a son. May they each be a tribute to the Starmark clan."

WARD

Before their short summer ended, a caravan arrived bringing more of Reaver's people to Wardenclave. Colonists. Men and women, outcasts and orphans, and if Pace's and Soon's excited descriptions were correct, a small group of Amaranthine.

"What kind?" asked Glint.

Soon sat back on his haunches. *"Not like us."*

Perhaps Glint shouldn't have been so grateful that no wolves had entered his territory. An interested female could have meant the swift fulfillment of his pact with Path.

As if lasting bonds were ever swift or easy.

Propping his hands on his hips, he glared up at the star dancing in the twilit sky. Rather than showing any sign of contrition over Glint's ever-lengthening wait, it blazed twice as bright as usual, as if celebrating the arrival of so many sparkling souls.

The newcomers were better warded and better armed, but if Glint could taste them on the wind, so could any determined tracker. He hoped the promised barrier wouldn't be long in rising.

Gerard strode forward with two other men and tried to initiate a proper introduction, but the darker of the two cut across his words to demand, "What have you done with the Twinned Child?"

Glint glanced at Gerard, trying to get a sense of what was happening.

"Waaseyaa," he explained. "He seems to be missing."

This was the first Glint had heard of Waaseyaa being a twin. "He has a sibling among you? I thought he was all alone." Inwardly, he ordered whoever among his Kith had the boy to bring him quickly.

"Coming!"

That was Trio, and Glint turned and smiled at the sight they made. Waaseyaa was riding on Trio's back, with three pups gamboling around his paws, doing their level best to trip up their father. Waaseyaa beamed as if he'd taught Trio a new trick.

"My pack is fond of the boy," said Glint in

mild reproach. "We watch over him."

"You *warded* him?" interrupted the other man, a flaxen-haired fellow with a pointed beard and eyes the hue of a morning sky. "I have never heard of a ward so ... *personal*! But how is it anchored?"

Before Glint could explain, the other one thrust out his hands, gruffly giving his name as Brings the Wind. "Please, forgive me. When I thought him gone, I assumed the worst. His loss would devastate our plans for Wardenclave. But to have found a place among wolves!"

"Dogs," Glint firmly corrected.

"I have never encountered a dog clan." Hemet was not a tall man, but he wasn't lacking in enthusiasm. "You are a ward? We found a warded farm on the edge of town. It must be yours—the warding, not the farm. Or *are* you a farmer?"

As Gerard did his best to explain a pack's presence in the middle of their village, Glint contemplated the newcomers, automatically relating them to animals of his acquaintance. Hemet was sturdy as a wild pony and just as prone to prancing. He wheeled and exclaimed and complimented every aspect of their view.

Brings the Wind had the bearing of a falcon and was equally inscrutable.

Both piqued his interest, but not with Waaseyaa's command. Compared to them, his boy burned like a small sun, and Glint could find no clan comparison. His first impression lingered still. Waaseyaa was an angel, and his presence was becoming increasingly entwined with Glint's feelings of strength and hope and purpose. If Soriel's message had sent him here simply so he could meet Waaseyaa, then his solitude and centuries were well spent.

Of the four Amaranthine who arrived with the caravan, the first to seek him out was from one of the moth clans. Linlu Dimityblest was lithe and soft-spoken, with short hair mottled in powdery shades of brown and cream. The irises of his large eyes were nearly the same color as his skin—cool as river clay and glossy with interest. "You are a wolf."

"I am a son of the packs," he conceded. "But anything made can be remade. I am a dog. The first of my clan."

"Do you know of enclaves?"

"Not by that name." Glint thought back to the discussions at his last few Song Circles. "Alliances between clans have always seemed wise to me, but the cooperatives I heard about formed to hide from human encroachment. You're building *with* them."

"Gerard is on a crusade, and we support his purposes."

"And what *are* those purposes?" Glint was glad for this chance of a more thorough explanation than limited vocabularies had previously allowed.

"The ancient groves are gone. The tree-kin are scattered. Our guide calls them a flock without a shepherd." Linlu's dainty hands fluttered. "We have gathered them up to give them safe haven. Wardenclave will be their home."

Glint eyed him with concern. "What safety can moths, rabbits, and squirrels offer?"

"Camouflage." Linlu reached out to catch Glint's sleeve. "But you are strong. Do you intend to remain with us here?"

"I'm here by the Maker's leading, but I'm not privy to His purposes. All I know for certain is that I cannot leave unless my star leads."

"Then we are similarly guided." Linlu lifted his face to the spark that could be seen faintly against the blue of the sky. "Gerard chose me because I am sensitive to Impressions."

Only children believed in lorefolk, the so-called lost clans. Glint might have been more skeptical of Linlu's claim if he hadn't been sent out by an angel to trudge across tundras in the wake of a star.

"They're twins, you know—those stars."

Glint had thought his star brighter. Perhaps it was, but only because it no longer danced alone.

Linlu said, "You are protecting the boy."

He grunted an affirmative.

"His soul is especially clear and sweet. The brightest I have seen in three generations." With a reverent tone, he added, "My people call those like Waaseyaa *beacons*. He pulls people like us toward him."

Again, Glint grunted.

"You are patient."

He frowned. "With the boy? He's a child."

"He's a tempting prospect. Those who pursue us haven't the patience to cultivate a community like ours and the communion it fosters." Linlu edged closer, his voice dropping. "Have you noticed a change within yourself since the boy entered your care?"

Glint inclined his head. "I have less difficulty forming sigils, and those I create are more effective."

"Your reserves will double and redouble, and in truest form, you will gain in both speed and stature." Linlu's hands flowed gracefully as he spoke. "Little by little, as you tend to such a child, they tend to you. Strength for protection. And greater protection due to increasing strength."

"An exchange of sorts," Glint mused.

"Mutually beneficial," he agreed. "However, some have no patience. Rather than nurture a potent soul, they snatch at strength, tearing and consuming. So many have been lost already. These humans are growing increasingly rare."

"So Gerard is collecting them to keep their kind from being hunted out of existence."

"Yes."

"Why bring them *here*?"

Linlu's laugh was a gentle vibration, like wind through leaves. "The Maker of one path can surely make another."

Glint remembered Linlu's mention of a guide and squinted into the sky. "I was visited by an angel called Soriel. Ever heard that name?"

"No." The moth clansman's expression softened. "Ours was Auriel."

Now *that* was a name Glint knew. "Auriel of the Golden Seed?"

"The very same." Linlu's hand drummed lightly over his heart. "I am glad to learn there is so much truth in the old tales. We may all be here to witness a dawning."

THREAT

Even though Glint had come from a different direction and without any intention of founding an enclave, Linlu Dimityblest included his name on the charter, and the other Amaranthine deferred to Glint as if he were their leader.

"You have more years," reasoned Bram Duntuffet, a fast-talking rabbit who excelled at foraging.

"And you have our support," added Colt Hannick Alpenglow, a healer whose cart was a rolling herbiary.

Glint's gaze lifted to the branch where the final Amaranthine member of Reaver's team lounged. Salali Fullstash pulled a floppy-brimmed hat low over his eyes. Based on the subtle strength Glint could sense lurking behind his lazy exterior, the squirrel clansman might have taken charge. In fact, he probably *had* over the course of their journey. But now that they'd arrived, Salali was only too happy to yield.

"Lead on, pooch." The gray-haired Amaranthine only smirked and waved off Glint's glare. "We'll call it 'divine right' and expect great things of you. No pressure."

Linlu's smile was far too pleased. "With your agreement, we will be unanimous."

Glint considered the moth, whose pen poised over the book he was already writing, a record of Wardenclave's founding. Maybe this was an honor. He should probably take it seriously. But it didn't feel like he was making history ... just picking up everyone else's slack. Even so, he mustered a bit of dignity. "I am where I belong. The people of Wardenclave may count on the Starmark clan's protection."

With a flourish of his pen, Linlu intoned, "So it has been agreed. So let it be done."

The attack came without warning—torrents and tremors. A battering began overhead, testing the strength of Hemet's barrier.

Something else was hitting low. Based on the noise of scrabbling and the shift and rattle of stones, Glint could only assume the wall itself was in danger. If their attackers pried away Hemet's sigil-bearing crystals, Wardenclave's defenses would fall.

"What are we looking at?" whispered Linlu, who blinked nearsightedly.

"Foxes," snapped Bram, who shifted a short club from hand to hand. "Same lot that picked up our scent two mountain ranges back."

"The wards?" asked Hannick.

"Holding," said Salali. "Barely."

Glint bit back a growl as Waaseyaa scrambled up the rise and barreled into his side. "I told you to stay with Path."

"I did. He came with me." The boy's gaze darted from wall to sky. "They found us again?"

Just then, Hemet took a stand midway between the center of town and the stone wall. With a chunk of crystal in each hand, he sent a wave of power outward. The initial crack set Glint's hairs on end, and an aftershock singed their tips.

"That smarts," muttered Bram.

Salali was already throwing up a defensive barrier. "Keep your whiskers on."

"What exactly did he do?" demanded Glint. He'd never seen a human capable of harnessing any portion of their soul. Admittedly, Reaver's people were fundamentally different—as different as his Kith were from their mothers.

"Hemet can create barriers, but he's even better with attacks. The crystals amplify his intent into an act of violence." Salali flashed a wry smile. "Don't underestimate these humans."

"Neither them nor cornered rodents." Glint braced himself against the backlash of another outburst. "Hasn't anyone tried refining his attack? If the crystal is his anchor, why not use it as a focus as well? Less waste. More damage."

Bram shot him an assessing look. "Spoken like a tribute. Were you set apart for war?"

"I'm not sure *why* I was set apart."

Salali's hands flashed, pulling complex patterns seemingly out of nowhere. As their lines snapped into place and gained strength, he drawled, "Is this *really* the time for a chat about sigilcraft and destiny? Refine later.

Survive now."

Glint scanned the wall, picking out the places where his own sigils held the line. "Waaseyaa, can you do things like that?"

The boy shook his head.

Bram said, "A shame, given his considerable resources."

"He doesn't respond to any of Hemet's crystals, either," said Salali, his voice tight. "Not to say there aren't other types we can tune, but remnants are a limited resource. We're hoping Bram will find more in these parts."

"Is this *really* the time for a chat about mountain lore and mining?" The rabbit's nose wrinkled and twitched. "Ward me, so I can get in there."

TEAM

Glint watched the humans rally and rush, using wave after wave of raw power to drive back the three foxes beyond their boundary. From his vantage, it wasn't hard to spot the weakness in their strategy. Hemet's attacks had a limited range, so all their opponents needed to do was pull back to a safe distance. Having determined the length of Wardenclave's tether, they dodged the brunt of every blast.

"He needs to get in closer," muttered Glint.

"True enough," conceded Salali. "But we cannot withstand Hemet's destructive force."

"Bram's doing well enough."

The squirrel offered a thin smile. "My warding only holds up for a little while—five, six blasts at best."

Glint's mind was reeling through ways to improve on their system. If Reaver's men and Amaranthine were to work in tandem, shielding might help, but focusing the attack would be better for everyone. It was an intriguing puzzle.

Pushing those thoughts aside for later, Glint said, "Those foxes are going to drag this out in order to wear Hemet down. We need him and his crystals up under their chins if we're going to wipe those grins from their faces."

"I'll do it!"

Glint turned, startled to find Trio pawing the grass. "Do what?"

"Let me carry the Reaver to the enemy." He barked for emphasis. *"It's my right. My pups are in danger."*

"As are mine," Glint gruffly reminded.

Trio's gaze didn't waver. *"Come with me."*

It wasn't a bad plan. With a resigned huff, he ordered, "Trio, carry Salali. Salali, be flashy. Create a distraction. Have Bram withdraw, and see if you can lure one of those pests into closer quarters. I'll carry Hemet."

"Simple enough. Ward yourself well." Then Salali was offering his palms to Trio, and they sprang away together.

"Waaseyaa, stay with Path. He'll protect you."

"With my life."

The boy knotted his fingers into Path's fur and whispered, "I promise."

Glint knew he could make use of the sigils already embroidered into his tunic. The wards would render him—and Hemet—hard to notice. Mindful of his promise to the Maker, he strolled into battle. Advancing at his ordained pace. Every step a choice.

Glint only looked back once, to make certain Waaseyaa was safe. He needn't have worried for the boy. Path had stayed back, as promised, but he also rallied his brothers to follow Glint's lead.

Rile now carried Brings the Wind. Pace and Soon also found partners from among Reaver's men. Young Edge had even charged in, presenting himself to Gerard.

Glint took the time to ignite several sigils and bolster his sons' defenses. He didn't like seeing his pack endangered, but the dogs were far more suited to war with foxes than the frighteningly vulnerable colonists.

"I'll carry you."

Hemet rounded on him, his face a mask of confusion.

Glint repeated, "I'll carry you. On my back. In truest form."

"Oh!" The man's grip on his crystals tightened. "Are you sure, Glint? I don't want to hurt you."

"Keep that thought foremost in your mind, and your soul won't consider mine a threat." He clapped the man's shoulder. "Don't worry, man. I've taken measures to protect myself and my dogs."

Hemet's gaze hardened. "Together, then!"

Transformation at close quarters left Glint and Hemet momentarily stunned, and for similar reasons. The man clearly hadn't expected to be facing such a large beast, and Glint hadn't expected to tower so far over the field. It took a moment to haul himself into tight enough control to maintain a size closer to that of his Kith, making it much easier for Hemet to climb aboard.

The proximity of the man's crystals and

conjurations rattled Glint to the very core of his being. But Hemet's searing attacks never turned on his mount. A promising sign. Reaver's men could be taught.

Under the cover of Glint's sigils, they made their way beyond the quavering barrier, and as soon as they were close enough, Hemet's power came crashing down on the nearest fox. The lone male dropped, killed outright, and the other two recoiled and retreated.

The dogs of the Starmark pack howled in defiance.

Reaver's men raised their fists and roared victoriously.

Not a soul lost.

Glint lifted his nose to the twin stars dancing in the evening sky and sang out a promise. To the Maker and his angels, to Reaver and his Amaranthine allies, to Waaseyaa and his packmates. Wardenclave was his to guard, and by the Maker, *all* its people would be safe.

Back in the safety of his den, Glint reassured himself by checking and brushing each of his children. Now that the brief skirmish was over, his heart lurched, and his hands trembled. As proud as he was of his sons, Glint quailed before the belated realization that any of them could have been hurt.

Worse, that possibility remained if the vixens they'd driven off proved vindictive.

Perhaps he should offer to work with Hemet. And Bram seemed to be a scrapper. Maybe the rabbit could show his Kith how to defend themselves while they defended the mountain.

Not until he'd finished brushing the smallest pup did Glint turn his attention to Waaseyaa. The boy had definitely caught his mood and remained quiet, curled into a tight ball between Path's forepaws.

"I haven't forgotten you." Glint beckoned.

Waaseyaa crawled forward, wide-eyed and wilted.

Gathering him up, Glint teasingly went through the motions, checking for injuries and chuffing the boy under his chin. He even loosened Waaseyaa's braid in order to brush out his hair, just as he'd done for his own.

The boy made a small noise of protest.

"No?"

Waaseyaa flushed. "I'm too old for this."

"How old are you supposed to be?"

"Practically grown!"

"Oho?" Glint hid his smile. "Well, *I'm* not too old for this, and I can boast centuries."

"How many?"

He paused to ponder. It was harder to keep track without marking every Song Circle. Finally, he guessed, "Four, I think."

"Truly?"

Glint chuckled. "I will go on and on for ages innumerable, but you are young. Be young."

Waaseyaa's dark eyes slowly filled with tears, and he curled into Glint. "Promise?"

"What pledge do you need from me?"

"Go on and on?"

"Is that all?" Glint kissed the boy's forehead. "That's how I was made. I can share all your years, Waaseyaa. Gladly."

The boy burst into tears and didn't stop until he'd cried himself to sleep.

"I don't understand." Path's voice was taut with concern and confusion.

"Strong emotions can lead to tears," murmured Glint. "Consider them a compliment. He's found a safe place to let them fall."

"But I thought tears were a mark of sadness." Path snuffled lightly. *"This scent is different."*

"I know." Glint brushed hair away from Waaseyaa's forehead. He'd been close to a similarly complex scent once before—when Bel told him of his suitor. "These were tears of joy."

SEED

Glint watched Waaseyaa wake, let him wriggle free to attend to his morning needs, and welcomed him back to the warmth of the pack ... all without a word. The boy crowded close, and Glint offered the smallest of hums to let him know he was listening.

With a sigh, Waaseyaa began, "I was born in a wood where trees still sang."

An old grove? Glint had never given much credence to the sagas of storytellers, but lore seemed to be springing to life all around him.

"I was born to be sent." Waaseyaa's voice was steady, sure. "I am part of the scattering."

Having himself been sent away from his home, Glint's hum held sympathy.

"I was ...." Waaseyaa looked up, searching Glint's face as he revealed, "I was born with a seed in my hand."

Glint blinked. Is *this* what Brings the Wind had meant, calling Waaseyaa a twinned child?

He quietly asked, "A golden seed?"

"Yes." The boy sat up and pulled at a cord around his neck. A small pouch hung from it, securely knotted. "I have a golden seed."

In the stories, such seeds were the blessing of Amaranthine trees. A child born holding one was meant to plant it and tend to their twin, and in exchange, they would share the tree's years.

Waaseyaa's tone wobbled. "My parents could not run when the foxes came. My aunts and uncles, my older sisters, my friends—they could not get away because they could not leave. We have always been tree-kin, and we share their roots."

No wonder he was rare. No wonder he had no rival. Glint tugged Waaseyaa back down, holding him gently, trying to give back a little of what he'd lost.

"I was afraid to plant it anywhere we've been since then." Waaseyaa looked away shyly. "Once I do, it will be forever. And that's a long time to be alone."

Glint understood then, and he knew what it meant for him. Even if his star were to move on, he would not follow. Not if it meant leaving Waaseyaa behind. "*All your years, boy,*" he pledged anew. "Gladly."

Waaseyaa tried to keep from smiling and failed. He hid his face with both hands only to giggle behind them. The whole pile woke to their father in a playful tussle with the boy whose happiness washed over their souls in heartening waves.

Near midday, voices approached the den, and Glint opened his door to Brings the Wind, who was arguing in hushed tones with Gerard. Even though he'd heard every word and knew their purpose, Glint held his peace.

"About yesterday." Brings the Wind's gaze sought and found Rile. "Your dog made a fine partner, and I do not see the harm in asking. What would you trade for one of them?"

Gerard was mumbling apologies, but Glint raised a hand.

"You've taken a liking to Rile?"

The man's eyes lit up. "I didn't know his name. A good name. Yes, Rile."

Glint turned to his son and asked, "And what do you think of this man?"

"Stubborn. Rash. Fearless." His jaw dropped in a doggish laugh. *"I like him."*

Brings the Wind had gone very still. "Why ask your animal for his opinion?"

"Rile is one of my Kith." Glint inclined his head toward Gerard. "As you've already been told, these dogs aren't merely intelligent. They are people."

"I thought it uncanny, the way he responded to my wishes during battle." Brings the Wind strode to Rile and flung his arms wide. "I am making a bad impression on the very one I want to impress. Will you forgive me?"

"See what I mean?" Rile was on the verge of laughter. *"He's not even afraid to admit he's a fool."*

Glint did appreciate honesty. And Rile's opinion mattered more than anyone else's on the matter. So he addressed himself to Brings the Wind. "He likes you."

Hope rekindled in the man's eyes, and he

reached for Rile. "You do?"

"He certainly does, and if he wants to spend time with you, I won't stand in his way." Glint tried not to show how much the words cost. "Rile is an adult and free to choose. If you can make peace with him, you will gain a lifelong friend."

A few years passed, and Wardenclave's foundations took shape. The encircling wall gained height and breadth, and the cleared space in the village center became a proper Song Circle. Colt Alpenglow sowed the wide meadow with fragrant grasses, and Bram helped him set saplings in a ring around its edge. Glint suspected that the original plan had been for Waaseyaa to plant his golden seed in the middle, but the boy's twin had taken root beside his den's door.

The Starmark pack expanded by several litters, and Kith had become something of a commodity. Glint chose not to discuss his role as parent to the first generation of Kith, who were now spending more of their time in various households throughout Wardenclave. Only Path remained a constant in the home den.

Children arrived in the village, some by birth, others because Gerard still searched for those touched by the power that set apart Reaver's people. Glint agreed with Linlu that the trait was hereditary, so he took an interest in bloodlines.

Glint was soon branded a matchmaker.

Not *entirely* fair, given his pragmatic streak. As far as he was concerned, the preservation of reavers—as he'd begun to call them— was served as much by propagation as by protection.

TIME

Waaseyaa surged through adolescence with a speed that unsettled Glint. After promising to be there for all his years, they seemed determined to slip away. His boy was a boy no longer. And his interests would soon lead him elsewhere. Not far, of course. But not *here*. With a pang of loneliness, Glint pulled Waaseyaa closer.

That earned him a grunt, and a sleep-husky voice asked, "What is it?"

"My pup has reached his attainment and will leave my den to make his own." He injected a piteous note into his complaint. "Is my loyalty not enough?"

A slim brown hand patted his. "You're a good friend, Glint, but you're not the one I've been courting."

"I cannot fault your preference for Hemet's daughter. Only your decision to take her elsewhere. You would have been welcome here."

Waaseyaa snorted. "That might have proven awkward."

"In what sense?"

The young man patiently pointed out, "There's only one bed."

"And I have always been willing to share it."

One eye opened. "Are you done teasing?"

Glint grumbled, "What kind of question is that?"

"A futile one. You *enjoy* teasing me."

"I will do so for as long as I can, if not longer." He rumbled his contentment. "I do not begrudge you your mate. Go to her. Be fruitful, multiply. May your progeny be many and bright."

"What about you?" asked Waaseyaa.

Not this again. "Have you been talking to Path?"

"You know I can't hear Kith voices."

Glint grinned. "A mercy, I assure you."

Waaseyaa pressed, "Couldn't we find you a mate? Bram and Linlu managed."

"That's entirely different. They were already promised before making their journey to Wardenclave." He mussed the young man's hair. "Secure your own happiness, for it has become mine."

When Waaseyaa became a father, he had barely achieved his second decade, which was typical of the other humans in the village. Wardenclave celebrated. Their beacon had a son. The future would be bright. All was as it should be.

A little more time passed, and Waaseyaa's wife gave him a second and a third child—both daughters—each a dazzling addition to the reaver community. However, with the arrival of a fourth child, Glint noticed a change. Or rather, a lack of change.

Waaseyaa remained a youth of twenty, while his wife grew worn by years of carrying and caring. People remarked, and her customary smiles grew strained. Affection faltered, and no more children were conceived. Glint tried to speak with her, but her hurt ran deep. Waaseyaa's joy faltered, and Glint found that sadness, too, could be shared.

In a few more years, Waaseyaa was almost

indistinguishable from his eldest son, and the rift became a chasm. Waaseyaa quietly moved back into Glint's den.

"You were raised among trees." Glint cradled the man who was no longer young, despite appearances. "Did you know this might happen?"

Waaseyaa nodded.

Glint swallowed further comment. His boy stank of heartbreak and regret. What use were should-haves and could-haves?

"I knew, but I loved her." He nestled closer. "I thought it would be enough."

He loosened Waaseyaa's hair as he used to, dragging his fingers through its length. His boy might not be growing any older, but his hair continued to grow. "Is this why you planted your seed beside my door instead of your own?"

"It was easier to be brave knowing that you would take me back." Waaseyaa hid his face and mumbled, "Did I betray her?"

"Have you been loyal to the one you chose?" Glint asked. Not because he needed to inquire, but because Waaseyaa needed reminding.

"I have!"

"You devoted yourself to her happiness and shared it?"

"I did." Emotions played across his face. "I still will."

Glint's heart ached for the boy. "You left for her sake."

"Yes." Waaseyaa's lips trembled. "It was the only thing she wanted. The only thing left to do."

Over the next few days, Glint told Waaseyaa about the dogs he'd taken to his heart over the years. Because they had each taught him the everyday truths he now lived by. Simple lessons. That he was not made to be alone. That lives are all the more precious for their brevity. That words have power, be they promises, songs, or names. That heartache was true love's twin. And that life and death and change were part of going on and on.

"Our children," Waaseyaa said, his smile

coming more easily. "We have fine children."

"None finer," Glint agreed. "Next time you take a wife, you must explain things carefully. She must know the consequences of wedding herself to tree-kin."

Waaseyaa looked stunned. "I *have* a wife, even if she doesn't want me. And I really don't think there can ever *be* a next time."

"Remain loyal," Glint agreed. "But by and by, you should take a new mate. If not for yourself, then for the sake of the village. Your children outshine those of every other reaver."

"I ... I can't." Eyes on the ground, he muttered, "Who would want such a husband?"

"You might be surprised." Glint took his chin, forcing Waaseyaa to lift his eyes. "You are strong and comely, and your children are the pride of Wardenclave. When the time comes, we'll have Linlu begin a registry so that the names of your wives will stand alongside yours for all time. You will live to see their strength and beauty passed on to future generations."

Waaseyaa spoke haltingly, pleadingly. "Even Sanne?"

Glint rumbled approvingly. "Honor her in your heart and in our history—Sanne, First of Wards."

MOON

Not many years later, in the midst of a restless winter's night, Glint paced Wardenclave's new perimeter, which encompassed a much wider swath of territory. Much of the Denholm range had effectually disappeared, thanks to an intricate combination of sigil-based illusions—anchored by crystals, powered by reavers. But Gerard's son and successor was a cautious man, and Glint was inherently protective of their home. Their guard never wavered.

As he walked through heavy woodland, casually checking each ward in passing, Glint met a reaver coming in the other direction—Brings the Wind's granddaughter astride Rile. He lifted his hand, and she reached down. Their fingertips brushed, the same shy greeting they'd exchanged since she was small.

"How goes the night watch?" he asked.

Summer Breeze peered back the way they'd

come, her lips pursed. "There is a wolf."

"I wouldn't worry. They'll catch the scent of the Demon Dogs of Denholm and steer clear."

"But Rile has been restless," she persisted. "He doesn't like this one, and it's getting closer."

"Oh?" Glint took his son's muzzle in both hands. "That's unusual."

"*That's no ordinary wolf,*" said Rile. "*He has a voice.*"

"You don't like the sound of him?"

Rile hesitated. "*I don't know. Maybe they are lost. Or lost someone. It worries me.*"

Glint turned his head in the direction Summer Breeze had indicated, senses straining.

"*I don't know if it's a word or a name,*" said Rile. "*But it sounds like he's calling ... Loor-ket.*"

He grunted in surprise.

"*Father?*"

Glint roughed up his son's fur and smiled at his rider. "Don't worry, Summer Breeze. I'll check on the wolf and see if it intends us any mischief."

He walked to the crest of one of Denholm's foothills, a hilltop meadow where they sometimes grazed their flocks and herds. The moon was new, which allowed the lesser lights to rule the long night. Half a lifetime ago, he'd walked away from his home, slowly chasing his choices across snowfields to this place. Would he need to answer for those choices now?

Glint folded his arms over his chest and set his jaw. He would stand by them.

Finally, a howl cut through the night. Glint hadn't realized how high his hopes had been until they came crashing down. It wasn't Bel. His brother hadn't come searching.

Why would he?

Glint couldn't begin to fathom who else might care enough to track a centuries-gone loner. But he filled his lungs and let loose with a shrill whistle.

The hunter wasn't even trying for stealth. At a crashing in the underbrush, Glint turned in time to see a wolf bound into the open, pale as moonlight, tail flagging eagerness and joy.

Not a member of the Highwind pack.

His mystification momentarily deepened when the wolf tumbled into transformation and kept running on legs no less roughened by fur. Those ears, that tail. In his final leap, the young male was reaching with clawed hands, but Glint didn't even try to defend himself, only braced himself for the oncoming collision.

The Kith-kin wasn't going for his throat.

Arms wrapped around his neck, and breathless laughter came with a husky chant. "Found you, found you, found you!"

"Moon-kin!" Glint returned the fierce hug, if a bit bemusedly. "Why are you here?"

"To find you." Moon stepped back and grinned with fierce triumph. "I had to keep my promise."

The scruffy whelp was gone, replaced by a fine figure of an adult—well-muscled and bristling with confidence. Moon was more animal than most Amaranthine, but he was clearly at ease in his form.

Startled, but glad, Glint pulled him into another embrace, welcoming him as he would a friend or packmate, ally or son.

"What a chase you must have had."

"You have no idea." Moon butted his head under Glint's chin, as if he were a pup again. "I've been searching for a long time."

He stroked the young man's hair and scratched affectionately behind canine ears. "Why would you need a loner like me?"

"I promised Marnoo."

Glint shook his head. "How is your fosterling?"

"She's strong, and her will is stronger." Easing from Glint's embrace, the young wolf drew himself up to answer more formally. "I am Marnoo-vel Ambervelte's go-between. She will have you and no other."

He stared blankly at Moon. Finally, he held up two hands, describing the size of the wolf cub he'd rescued so many years ago. "Your half-sister."

Moon lifted a hand, indicating a height close to his own. "My half-sister."

Glint rubbed at his forehead. Cubs did grow, and the centuries were sufficient to have brought Moon and Marnoo to adulthood. But this made no sense. "I met you once and briefly. We shared stories in a snowbank until you fell asleep, and I carried you to your people. That's all."

"You made a lasting impression."

On a cub not even weaned? Glint was increasingly perplexed. "That was never my intent."

"Yet to Marnoo, you are the scent of stars, the voice of an angel, and the hope of all her somedays." Moon searched his face, utterly serious. "Are you bonded to another? Promised?"

"No, there is no one here. I am ... well, I'm not *alone*." Glint didn't know where to begin. "My situation is complicated."

"Complexities are not objections." Moon's eyes sparkled. "Tell on!"

Glint bluntly stated, "I have no tail."

"I noticed."

"I'm no longer a wolf." Chin lifting, Glint announced, "I'm a dog."

Moon waited for several beats, then asked, "Tamed and tailless? Is that all?"

"No. I have a clan ... allies ... responsibilities."

"A clan? Do you want to appoint a go-between as well?" His ears swiveled as a voice reached the both of them.

"I will speak for my father." Path strolled into the open, head high and proud. *"He is Glint Starmark, First of Dogs, Friend of Beacons, Founder of Wardenclave."*

Glint huffed at the stiff boast and gestured between them. "This is my eldest son Path. I have become a Kith-sire."

"I am Moon-kin Ambervelte." He hurried to Path. "My half-sister is full-blooded like your father, and he is her choice. Would the pack accept her pursuit?"

"Wholeheartedly." Path touched his nose to Moon's brow. *"The stars have been singing about you. I didn't realize the* chasing moon *would be a wolf."*

The Kith-kin's tail wagged. "Our coming was foretold?"

Our. Glint had thought Moon was alone. He cast about with his senses.

Moon went right on, "If I am the moon, then Marnoo is its radiance."

Why did those words sound familiar?

And ... someone was nearby. He could feel

a close-kept presence, like a huntress on the prowl. But before he could decide what to do, Moon was standing before him, proffering a small cloth-wrapped parcel.

Glint gasped and took it with reverent desperation. Because it smelled like his twin.

COMB

A betrothal gift," said Moon. "Prepared for Marnoo-vel by Beloor-dex Ambervelte with every blessing ... and a promise."

Glint slowly unfolded the rippling copper cloth, which concealed a comb—a traditional courting gift—decorated with delicate clusters of stars. His brother's own handiwork. An intensely personal gift.

Moon spoke gently. "If you wish it, he will come to stand by your side and bear witness to your bonding."

"Bel would come here?"

"He has promised it."

Glint's emotions were already a mess when Moon's and Path's gazes swung to the same spot. A white wolf stepped into the open. She'd been a pretty cub, but Glint never would have recognized the oncoming she-wolf as that whimpering fuzz ball. *Beautiful* fell short. Marnoo was exquisite—fine-figured, graceful, and direct. He couldn't look away from those astonishing copper eyes, even as she took speaking form.

"Hello," he offered a little breathlessly.

She prowled around him, looking him over, testing the air, taking her time.

Glint flushed, suddenly conscious that he wore his shabbiest breeches and scuffed boots. Having rolled out of bed to stalk the perimeter, he was unbrushed, unkempt, and probably smelled strongly of Waaseyaa.

But Marnoo paused to trail her finger along the ornate embroidery decorating his tunic. Approval shone in her gaze. "You are arrayed as finely as a lord at his bonding feast. And those you keep closest have covered you in the scents of peace, trust, and power."

He was utterly tongue-tied.

"That's good, right?" Path asked, *"Now what?"*

Marnoo's lips curved. "Glint Starmark, First of Dogs, Friend of Beacons, Founder of Wardenclave, has my journey been worthwhile? Or will you send me into solitude?"

Glint sort of figured that her options weren't quite so limited. Nor was she any more alone than he was. Moon was a solid presence, looking on with an indulgent expression. But Glint knew what she meant, so he said, "It's not good to be alone."

Path asked, *"How do we accept?"*

"An exchange," prompted Moon.

Marnoo eased into Glint's personal space, touched his cheek, then placed a staggeringly possessive kiss on his lips. "If you can tame me, I will take your name. If you claim me, our clan will increase in strength and beauty."

She was quite ... charismatic. Glint felt a little cornered and entirely outmatched. But humbled by this latest gift from the Maker's hand. With the music of stars teasing at the far reaches of his senses, he tucked his brother's gift into his sash in order to reach for her hands.

Low and gruff, he said, "For a gift. May I give you a name?"

Her brows arched. "Choose well."

Glint pressed his lips to her forehead, lingering there, savoring the moment. Was this how it was for Bel, being chosen, having a choice? When Glint drew back, he was astonished to see a tiny silvery star marked her brow. Had it always been there?

No.

His heart swelled with awe and pride. His mark. His mate.

She tilted her chin invitingly, so he kissed her lips. Everything was happening so fast—finding, feeling, falling. But his blood sang a true note, and she whispered encouragement. So Glint Starmark faced his future and gave her a name. "Radiance."

TREE

Several decades had passed since Waaseyaa planted the golden seed beside Glint's front step. Neither of them had known quite what to expect. Under Waaseyaa's careful watch, the tree took to earth and sky, gaining height with surprising speed, then doubling and tripling its girth until they had to move the threshold.

Glint tried to salvage the den by removing one wall, but the antiquated structure teetered into a heap that was little better than kindling. Radiance eagerly suggested a few changes when they rebuilt, and Glint belatedly realized that his bondmate was a patient, uncomplaining soul. They'd been living in a crowded shed for far too long.

With an eye to the future, they designed a spacious home with two ways in. One faced the village, a public entrance to the clan home of one of Wardenclave's five Amaranthine founders. The second entrance remained private, with its threshold resettled at what Waaseyaa deemed a safe distance from his tree.

Here, Waaseyaa had a little home of his own, looking out over the same old pasture where Glint still romped with the new generations of Kith pups born to the pack. Both the pasture and the tree towering over it were still heavily warded against notice. Thanks to Salali's expertise, citizens of Wardenclave tended to forget that Waaseyaa's twin dominated the mountaintop.

Once they were sure of the variety, Linlu Dimityblest disappeared for several seasons, traveling to one of the secret communities where the remnants of ancient groves clung to life. Without ever saying where he'd been or how he'd managed it, the moth clansman returned with five children in tow. Each wearing a special pendant, each carrying a golden seed.

The Alpenglow clan prepared homes at a modest distance from the Starmark holdings—three hilltops over and downwind. The horse clan became companions and caretakers for the children, whose plantings were the beginnings of a new grove.

"Why not closer to Waaseyaa?" grumbled Glint. "Two of them are girls; one of them might have made a good bride."

Linlu nodded sympathetically. "Who knows how much havoc one tree may cause? *Especially* if Waaseyaa's twin manifests as a female. Better to watch and wait, lest we take an unwise step."

Glint paused and paled. "Do you mean to say that the stories about the fruit of an Amaranthine tree are true?"

"Quite … efficacious," Linlu said mildly.

"And the pollen itself?" he asked, gazing warily up into the branches overshadowing his home.

"Intoxicating." With a soft smile and a suggestive hand gesture, he added, "Invigorating."

"How often does it bloom?"

"The interval is usually five years."

Glint cleared his throat. "Is *this* the reason more than half of the females in the village are carrying?"

"Your bondmate included." Linlu laughed

softly. "Congratulations."

He wasn't entirely sure why he should be so embarrassed. Linlu's family saw such regular additions, they already boasted a tribute. "A baby boom can only benefit the community."

"Agreed. The reavers are no longer in danger of disappearing, and the tree-kin have found another safe haven." The moth's gaze lingered on the large tree. "We are making a difference."

That same autumn, the cry came.

"Glint! Glint, I need you!"

There were times when it was difficult for Glint to maintain his self-imposed pace, but he managed to keep to an admittedly brisk walk in answer to his boy's call. Bursting through his back door, he stumbled to a halt before Waaseyaa.

He sat amidst roots that rose in smooth swirls, tangling around Waaseyaa's customary spot as if creating a throne for him. And he was hugging a naked child with a headful of blossoms where his hair should be.

Waaseyaa's eager expression told Glint every-thing, but he still asked, "What have we here?"

"My brother woke up."

The child was a beauty, with skin like fine-grained wood and thick-lashed eyes with a decidedly seductive tilt. Outwardly, he couldn't have been older than six, but Glint could tell he'd be trouble once he grew into the saucy allure for which storybook trees were famed.

Glint crouched before the pair and reached out to gently touch the cascade of sunset orange petals.

The tree-child caught and kissed his hand.

"Affectionate," Glint remarked.

Waaseyaa's lips quirked. "Extremely."

Glint sat on the ground, held out both hands, and found himself with his arms around a fabled imp. Would wonders never cease? "Do you have a name, boy? Or must I guess?"

"Brother named me." With a flash of dimples and a flutter of lashes, he sweetly said, "I am Zisa."

"It means *orange*," Waaseyaa murmured. "Welcome, Zisa. We've been waiting for you."

"I know." The child was suddenly nose-to-nose with Glint. "I know *everything*."

Glint rolled his eyes toward Waaseyaa. "Precocious."

"Endearingly."

Waaseyaa showed every sign of being smitten with his impish counterpart. That was good. He needed a distraction, and Zisa seemed the sort of boy to ... well, to demand too much attention. Glint decided that counted as a family resemblance.

"Here, I have kept my word." Glint couldn't help feeling relieved by the wild beat of Path's tail against the ground. Slouching into the Kith's bulk, he showed off his newborn son, swaddled in a blanket he'd embellished himself, its frippery and flourishes only partially disguising the protective sigils he'd worked into the soft cloth Radiance had loomed from several brushings of the Starmark clan. "I think there's a resemblance."

Thick auburn fuzz was already long enough to curl over ears that came to perfect points.

"My brother." Path sounded awed.

"Yes. You and he are both firstborn." Glint looked up into Path's face. "You each bear a great responsibility to our pack."

"Did you name him?"

"Oh, indeed." Glint tickled the pup's cheek, encouraging him to open copper eyes.

The little one's nose twitched, his lips pursed, and without any additional warning, he opened his mouth and howled.

Path was snickering, and Glint chuckled as well.

"Did you call him Noisy?"

"Apt though your suggestion may be, it's too late. Radiance and I agreed. We've named him for the future. This is Harmonious."

THE END

A Song for
Moon

1

SONG AND MOON

Moon knew he was beautiful. Everyone said so. It was in their songs and in their words and in the gentle way they tugged at his ears. Even before he sorted out how to open his eyes, he knew, knew, knew his favorite things. The safe place at his mother's belly and the milk that made him warm and sleepy. The hand that slowly stroked him from the top of his head to the tip of his tail, over and over and over again in a soothing rhythm. And the rumbling grumble that accompanied a voice that wove its way into his heart and stirred his tail against the straw.

"Where's my little tracker? Where is Song's good boy?"

Oh, he loved this voice. Moon was sure that of all the good things he'd found so far, best, best, best of all was Song.

If Mam was gone, Song was there, crooning

over him or bathing his face.

After one such washing, Moon opened his eyes.

"Well, hello, cub of my heart." A white wolf with blue eyes pricked his ears. *"Look closely, and breathe deeply. You should know me, for I am your Song."*

Moon whined and wriggled onto his back, paws reaching. *"Song, Song, Sonnnggg."*

Song lowered his muzzle and nudged Moon's belly. *"Finding your voice already, little one?"*

"Has he now?" And there was someone else leaning over him. "Bright boy."

Moon blinked up at a smiling face framed in hair that was dark gray and silver-tipped. His gaze was soft, and oh, Moon knew, knew, *knew* these gentle hands. He licked warm fingers and searched for a word for him. He didn't have one and whined.

"He has our Shinoo's eyes."

His rumble was lighter than Song's, but Moon liked it almost as much. *"Song, Sonnnggg,"* he tried.

"Song is your sire. Is he your favorite, then?

I'm also part of your family. Can you say Da, beautiful Moon?"

And so Moon's first word was Song, and his next was Da.

Only later did he learn that his den was different than most. Nobody else had two fathers, even though it helped, since they had so many more cubs—both Kith and Kindred—than any other den in the Ambervelte pack.

The one time Moon questioned it, his mother had stiffly asked, "Are you unhappy with your da or your sire?"

Moon was shocked she'd even ask. His fathers were best, best, best.

"Then are you unhappy with *me*?"

He gazed into copper eyes and honestly said, "We all love our Shinoo."

Only later did he learn that nobody else called their mother by name. But that was what Da and Song called her, and Moon knew they liked it when *he* did, too. Because Shinoo-dex Ambervelte was beautiful. Everyone said so. Beautiful ... and strange.

2

STRANGE DEN

Being Kith, Moon grew more swiftly than Kindred babies. While they wobbled and squalled, he found his feet and used his nose and learned to sing. Weeks added up to maturity, insight, and increased understanding.

He noticed things.

Like the way their den was situated way off at the far end of Ambervelte territory.

Like the stilling or tucking of tails whenever their Shinoo strode past other she-wolves.

Like the way gazes slid to the side whenever he spoke about one of his half-sisters or full-brothers or siblings from the wild mothers that Da had claimed.

He noticed, and he grew watchful.

Finally, he went to Song. *"Other dens are different."*

"Not so different," he countered. *"Denmates*

are dear to every heart, and we all have a part in the song."

Moon wasn't a baby anymore. *"I want to know."*

"Then I will tell you." Song made Moon curl up between his paws, and he spoke in a low voice that was only for him. *"Our Shinoo is precious to the Maker, for she was born a tribute. She is a strong protector, skilled in battle. Nobody wanted her, and she wanted nobody."*

"But she has us!"

"In her younger years, before your da came to us from the Brookwild pack, she was always alone. And too stubborn to admit that she was lonesome."

"Oh, nooo," Moon whined. *"Where were you?"*

"I was there. Always there. My sire was Shinoo's mentor. She came to our den to learn her duties to the Maker and to the pack. Shinoo and I became friends."

Moon wished he had a friend. *"And you became her Song?"*

"Yes. But we sang together in secret. When she was carrying our first litter, her mentor tried to help. He asked for another tribute to come, and so Brook arrived."

"Da."

"Yes. Brookwild-dex Brookwild came to add his strength to the Ambervelte pack."

"Does that mean ... bondmate?"

"It means breeding. *Like my own sire, your da is a Kith-sire. He was supposed to help Shinoo keep me a secret, but Brook disagreed with my sire. He supported my claim and called me her bondmate.*" He warmly added, "*He didn't think our love strange.*"

"Strange?"

"*It's unusual for any of the Kindred to choose a Kith partner.*"

"*Is that why the she-wolves stare?*" Moon thought it was a silly reason.

Song gently nipped Moon's ear. "*The staring began when Shinoo gave birth to your half-brother Koonta-soh.*"

"Why?"

"*Because his birth made our den strange. Because* Brook *is Koonta's sire.*"

Moon already knew that. Koonta's scent and coloring made that obvious. He was so much like Da. "*Koonta isn't the only one. So are Soora and Hiloo and Ranoo and Ooren and ...*

and the rest."

"Yes. Brook has impish ancestry, so our family has grown more swiftly than the others. There is no Waning for a child of storms." Song sounded proud, even pleased. *"We are strong, but some have a hard time understanding a she-wolf with two bondmates."*

"Is she the only one with two?"

"The only one."

"So that's why our den is different."

"Not so different," Song repeated warmly.

"But bigger," said Moon.

His sire chuckled. *"Yes, we're always getting bigger."*

3

LITTLE TRACKER

Moon woke with a start and peered around.

He'd dozed off his dinner curled among the homey heaps of dry grasses and thick blankets in the Kith shelter. This had been his haven ever since weaning. Usually, the space was crowded with Kith, for Da had brought many cubs down from the mountains over the years, and this was their haven, too. But there was nobody around. Not even Song.

His sire usually stayed with him, yet Moon was alone. And he wanted to know why, why, why. Should he find out? He was bigger now. He could handle it.

Padding to the entrance, Moon peered out into a moonless night, ears pricked. No wolves sang, but he caught a short, sharp yip in one direction. Then an answering *wuff*.

The patter of running paws.

A rustle in the long, dry grasses.

Nothing about the scents or sounds held fear. Only excitement and the sense of shared secrets. Did the older Kith play while cubs slept? Moon drifted further from the shelter, nose to the ground, seeking his favorite scents.

Da's was easy to find. He regularly visited the house that Shinoo used when she wanted privacy for training or for sleep. This house was also where Moon had been born. Breathing in the familiar scents, he followed the freshest in the direction Da had gone.

He found Song's scent next. Wanting to be with him, Moon followed their trail at a lope.

Other wolves were in the woods, and he recognized their scents. Other Amberveltes. Kith and Kindred. All of them males.

What kind of game was this?

Or maybe training?

He didn't like being left out. Even if he *was* youngest, he was a quick learner. Hadn't Song praised his tracking? Following scents was easy, easy, easy. Especially these scents. Da was with Song. Their paths crisscrossed, weaving as they'd run together. Moon followed through autumn-crisp woods, his heart light. This wasn't one of the paths he usually took, but the scents of his fathers were so clear, Moon didn't feel alone anymore.

He found them in the foothills, far from the encampment. A white wolf and a storm-gray wolf who was dark enough to be his shadow.

Just as Moon expected, they were playing. Frisking around each other in a dance that was part chase, part tussle. Breathy *wuffs* were like whispers. Moon couldn't hear them from his hiding place, and he couldn't quite place the scent on the air. The hot muskiness of it was half-familiar, and it made him curious.

Song grumbled around a mouthful of Da's thick ruff of fur. All of them were gaining the heavier coats that Song said they'd need in winter.

More nipping and circling, lunging and pouncing. Da's laugh sparkled, and Song uttered a word Moon didn't recognize, but it had a nice sound. So it was a good sort of word. Or a secret name.

All at once, Moon realized that this place

might be a little like Shinoo's house, some-where Song and Da went for privacy. Did that mean Moon wasn't welcome here? Would his fathers tell him to stay out like Shinoo had?

Grown too big to suckle. Growing too big for her little house.

Maybe Song and Da would say Moon was too little for games in the night. Should he ask? Would it be bad to interrupt them when they were so happy? He wanted to tell them that he was happy, too. That he was happy when they were happy.

Moon's tail swished, and he was reaching out, trying to think what to say.

"Me, too …?"

The words surprised a whine out of Moon.

Song's head turned.

But Moon was staring at the hand that was reaching out. It was his paw, but wolves didn't reach with their paws. Paws were for running. Except Moon's paw had changed. It was more like Da's hand.

Moon curled fingers and felt claws dent the skin of his palm. Flexing his fingers, he did it again. It felt strange, but not bad.

"Well, hello, cub of my heart." Song dropped onto his belly before Moon, his muzzle on his paws, his tail flagging. *"Did you have something to say?"*

Reaching out with both hands, Moon said, "I want to dance, too."

Words. A voice. His mouth had changed. Moon ran his tongue along the point of a tooth before speaking in a rush. "Don't stop. I like games, too."

"Moon?" Da hurried over on two legs. He breathed, "Look at you."

Song asked, *"Can you believe it?"*

"I'm amazed. I've *heard* of Kith-kin, but they're as fabled as imps."

"Your sire was a storm," Song blandly countered.

With a quirking smile, Da said, "Maybe that's why I am the way I am. And why I've always loved miracles. Come here, Moon."

Shuffling out of his hiding place, he stumbled forward, grabbing hold of Da's hands for support.

Warm fingers found his ears and tugged them in the usual way. Then Da ran his hand down Moon's back which was ticklish in new ways because there was so much bare skin. Moon's tail stirred and he dug the claws on his hind feet into the ground to help him balance. "This is me?"

"You're still our Moon," promised Song, whose voice was right where it had always been. *"You've taken speaking form."*

Da was kneading his thumbs into Moon's bare palms. "How do you feel?"

"Small. And … bare." After some thought, he admitted, "Sort of tippy. And strange …? Did I do it wrong?"

"Not at all."

And just as they had when he first heard their voices, they told him he was strong and beautiful and precious. Da rubbed their noses together, which brought Moon's new nose to his attention. Did he still look like Song? Maybe he looked like Shinoo now?

Moon was proud that his hands could be as gentle as Da's, and he gave his very first hug to Song. "Am I still your good boy?" he asked.

Song's tongue dabbed his forehead. *"You are and always will be. I'm so proud."*

"Won't our Shinoo be surprised?" Da asked with a laugh.

Moon was so happy that they were happy, which reminded him. "Is your game fun? Can I play, too?"

"Ah." Da glanced at Song. "We can play games anytime. Lots of new ones, I think, since you'll be training with me for a while. You'll need to get used to moving around in speaking form."

Song nipped Da's shoulder.

Da's smile went all crooked.

Like they were having a private conversation. And for the first time it occurred to Moon that Shinoo wasn't the only one with two bondmates. He looked to his sire and said, "You love Da."

"Yes, cub. He's part of me, and I'm part of him."

And searching Da's eyes, he checked, "You love Song?"

"So you noticed. Bright boy."

"Is this place ... secret?"

"Mmm. Not exactly. It's a place with good memories, so we come here from time to time."

Moon wasn't sure Da was telling the whole

truth. He looked to Song for confirmation.

"There's no harm in telling him. Moon is old enough to know."

Da looked flustered.

Rumbling with amusement, Song went on. "We were celebrating, cub. And you should be glad, too. You are going to be a big brother."

4

BIG BROTHER

Babies sure do take a long time," Moon grumbled.

"*It does seem that way, especially for Kith,*" said Song. "*Because of our heritage, we mature quickly. Our times are different. But rushing ahead means you'll be a capable big brother when Shinoo gives birth.*"

Was this impatience because he'd been born Kith?

Moon could count seasons as well as the next person.

He understood the passage of days and years.

Shifting into speaking form, Moon conceded, "Kith are really fast about reaching their attainment. But what about Kith-kin?"

They both looked to Da. As a dex, he should know.

He slowly shook his head. "There's no pattern. What little I've learned makes me think that you found your way into your speaking form especially young. That may be why you still look like a child, even though we're prepared to acknowledge your attainment."

Moon stood straighter. "My attainment?"

"Do you think you're not ready?"

"I am!" he yelped, worried they'd take it back. "I'm grown up inside, even if I look small."

"*We know, cub,*" Song assured. "*And we—all three of us—will acknowledge your attainment … and reward it.*"

"This child. Your new sibling," said Da. "We want you there. The baby will be born into your hands."

"*Because you* have *hands,*" whispered Song. "*Because you're Kith-kin, you can do this. You can have this.*"

Moon looked between them, uncertain. This was new. He didn't know what it meant.

Da explained, "You will foster your sibling as one of their parents. They will be a child in your den."

"I'll have a den?"

"It will be established," Da promised.

"Do I have to … go?" Moon didn't want to. Not at all.

"Nooo, *cub of my heart*," soothed Song. "*Never that.*"

"Stay and add to our strength," urged Da. "We'll dote on this new little one together."

5

INTO HIS HANDS

M*am?"* Moon whimpered.

He barely ever used his baby name for her—he was that used to calling her Shinoo—but it slipped out.

"Here, Moon-kin," she answered warmly. Well, warmly for her, since there was no underlying growl. Only a weary welcome that barely stirred her tail.

His own tail tucked in response, and he groveled on his belly in the straw.

"Afraid?" she quietly challenged. *"There's no need. You were born in this same room. Use your nose. Remember."*

Song settled beside him and nipped his ear. *"Listen, too. The sky is in a clamor. Can you hear it?"*

Moon tried to lift his ears, but they quickly drooped. He wasn't afraid. Not really. But his instincts were in a dither, and he was worried.

Da was sure that Shinoo was carrying more than the usual twins. She'd safely delivered three cubs before, but a runt didn't always thrive.

"*Can't you hear them?*" asked Song, his words just for him.

According to Da's stories, the farther north you traveled, the better your chances of catching a glimpse of an Impression. Ambervelte territory was in a temperate place, but the evening sky had been busy with setting sunbeams and gaining starsong. Even if wolves were meant to favor moonbeams, other lorefolk were just as good at leaving a soul breathless.

"*I can hear them. A little. More than I used to. But I can't piece together their lyrics.*"

"*Whenever our Shinoo gives birth, the heavens surround us.*"

"*Because of her heritage?*"

"*I think so.*" Song nuzzled him. "*Your birth caused just as much of a ruckus.*"

"*Ranoo said he was born in a storm.*"

"*Most of Brook's children were born with the scent of rain heavy in the air.*"

"Why not tonight?"

"Who can guess?" Song's gaze turned toward the entrance. *"Maybe so the stars can bear witness."*

Shinoo growled, and Da's tail swung higher.

Moon shivered at the shifting of scents. He loved his mother. According to Song, she was very good at having babies, in part because her mother was a moonbeam. Da had similar allure, and his heritage showed clearly in the first cub that slipped into his hands. They had his same darker fur.

"A son," Da announced, placing the little one between Song's forepaws.

Song licked the newborn until he protested with a squeaky howl.

Moon giggled. "He's cute."

"Careful, cub of my heart. This boy won't thank you if he's named for his adorability. Better to praise the strength he'll add to the pack."

"How do you pick names?"

Song's tail thumped. *"That's a question you should be asking yourself, Moon-kin. Since you'll be naming one of these cubs."*

"I will? But I don't know how!" Moon's mind

raced over the names of other wolves in their pack. This was so important. Why hadn't Da and Song told him sooner?

He was so worried, he almost missed the birth of a second cub.

"A daughter," declared Da, wiping the muzzle of another dark gray newborn. He crooned over her for several moments, then passed her along to Song.

"Show the elder brother to our Shinoo," urged Song. *"She'll want to see."*

Moon shifted and hefted the little boy—who repeatedly licked his chin—then carefully placed him where Shinoo could see. But her eyes stayed closed.

Fretting a little, he whispered, "Mam?"

Copper eyes drifted open. *"Did you forget my name?"*

He blushed. *"You're our Shinoo."*

"I like that. You're the first to ever dare. Brave boy," she murmured, nosing his hair. *"I wanted to name you Puff, you were so soft."*

Moon was surprised and a little horrified. Puff was almost as bad as Cute, not that his newborn brother would be given a Kith name. He was Da's boy, so it was certain that he'd find his way into speaking form one day.

"I like being Moon."

"Moon-kin," she corrected. They'd added to his name once they realized that he was Kith-kin. The change was small, but the added notes sang well. Moon liked the addition.

"Show me your hands."

Moon scooted closer, lifting bare palms.

"Good," she said. *"Now use those small hands to wrest a treasure worth holding."*

He dared to touch her face, hoped his smile didn't tremble too much, and whispered, "I'll love this baby with everything I have."

His mother rumbled another, *"Good."*

"Bring the little fellow over here," called Da.

Moon managed a respectable rumble as he lugged the cub to their mother's flank, where his littermate was already working out how to latch on. She was enough like the boy to be his twin. Moon fleetingly wondered what it would have been like to have a close sibling. But ... maybe if he'd grown up with a twin, he wouldn't have been quite so close to Song.

Could he be just as dear to the cub he'd foster?

He hoped so.

He'd make sure.

"Come here, Moon." Da's eyes were bright with delight as he patted the straw. "It's time. Here's your place."

Heart jumping, Moon stumbled into position and mostly collapsed there.

Da's hand plunked onto his head, tousling between his ears before stroking down over the storm-gray fur vest he wore. It reminded Moon of being petted when he was tiny. Turning in place, Moon flung his arms around Da's neck, nuzzled his jaw, and whispered a shy, "Thank you. I'll try to be as good as you."

With a low laugh, Da said, "You're as ready as anyone ever is for this. And you won't be alone in caring. Song and I will lend you our support."

Then things happened so fast.

Moon had to focus hard so he wouldn't forget a single moment of this child's birthing. Because he would be the one to sing of it later, when he shared this newcomer's name with the rest of the pack.

"A girl," he managed, gathering and nuzzling

and crooning. The rest were quiet, because his voice was meant to be the first she knew. His warmth and his touch and his scent.

White fur, like his. A moon-blessed child.

But oh, she was so tiny. Half the size of her siblings, at least.

Would she be all right? Could he make sure of it?

Cradling her close, he spoke in thoughts that were just for her. Because he knew just what to say. *"Hello, cub of my heart."*

6

MOON AND STARS

Once the newborn's belly was full of milk and she'd dozed off while he stroked her back, Moon carried the sister who would be like a daughter to him outside. "Just us," he whispered.

A thin skimming of snow broke under his paws with each step, but the sky was clear, and the stars were especially brilliant. His breath curled away in slow puffs. He'd always liked singing on nights like this, when steam mingled with each note before drifting toward the listening moon.

"Us and the sky," he quietly amended. It felt overly full tonight, like there were more stars than usual.

Now for a name. It must be a good one. True to her beginnings, but suited for her future.

He was Song's Moon. What would this girl be for him?

Born to the singing of stars that kept ringing in his ears, just out of range, indistinct and hinting at portents. Maybe ... maybe the best thing he could give this girl was the same thing he'd been given. A name that tied him to the one who'd always been best, best, best.

It was so much harder to sing in speaking form. Words were good, but a wolf's name sounded best when it was sung. *Da, may I borrow your hands? Song, will you stand with me and hear me sing?*

His fathers stepped outside.

Moon yielded the baby to her sire's keeping, then turned to bury his hands in Song's thick ruff, hugging hard before shifting into truest form. Sitting back on his haunches, he drew breath and sang the name he'd chosen, long and sweet and clear.

Da knelt, his eyes brimming. "It's a fine name, Moon."

"It resonates well," agreed Song.

Returning to speaking form, Moon took back the cub and announced, "Your name is Marnoo-vel." Because her name was his answer to the clamoring sky, for both the moon and for the stars to mark, since they'd been so noisy. He was claiming this sister for his den, and he'd raise her as he'd been raised. "You are my song. A song for Moon."

7

SONG'S TRIBUTE

Song Circles were held once every ten years, and according to Da, the one that the Ambervelte pack attended was hosted by the Highwinds, whose territory was far to the north. Moon wondered and worried about it, but nobody questioned that *everyone* should go, even Shinoo and her newborn cubs.

"Our Shinoo has responsibilities as a dex," explained Da. "And the Song Circle is a chance to see siblings who've had their strength added to other packs. We'll introduce you and Marnoo."

"And sing of your attainment," added Song.

So they packed for a journey. Da showed Moon how to bind Marnoo snug against his chest, where she'd be safe and warm. Da carried Hynoo and Jinyoo in the same way, with clingy Jinyoo snug against his chest and a contented Hynoo pressed to his back.

Along the way, Moon checked, "You'll introduce me as yours? Or as Kith-kin?"

"We'll have the chance to sing your whole story. Your birth. Your first name. Your new name. Your attainment." Da walked with a spring in his step and a swing in his tail. "All of it!"

Later, when they paused so that Shinoo could feed the cubs, Moon sought out Song. "Is being Kith-kin enough?"

Song's ears cocked in confusion. *"What do you mean?"*

"Being Kith-kin isn't my role in the pack."

"You're a fine tracker," Song pointed out.

Moon *had* reached the goal first during a recent Ambervelte trial, but he shook his head. "Is being a tracker enough?"

"Is it not enough?"

"No, I don't think it is."

His sire pondered that. *"You're a parent now."*

"Yes, but that's more about Marnoo than me." At least, that's how it felt. Moon struggled to find the right words to explain what he meant. "I want something that will always be mine."

"Ohhh." Sounding slightly awkward, Song ventured, *"Maybe it's too soon for that sort of thing?"*

Moon didn't see how. He wasn't ready to give up on getting his meaning across. "What do you have that's enough?"

"I have Shinoo," Song said gently. *"And I have Brook. Even if other things alter or grow apart, our bond is the truest of true things in my life. And that's always been enough for me."*

Moon was the tiniest bit hurt that he wasn't included among Song's best things, but hadn't Moon just said that being a parent wasn't enough? If Marnoo wasn't his all, then Moon couldn't be Song's all. "Will I have a bondmate?"

His father turned the question around. *"Do you want a bondmate?"*

"Not sure." With a shrug, he said, "Not just yet."

Song's jaw dropped in a wolfish laugh. *"It is a little early to be giving chase."*

"Being a tracker is something all of us do. Even if I'm faster, I'm not any different than the others." With a sigh, Moon said, "It must be nice for Da and our Shinoo. They have unique duties because they're both dexes."

"*I think ...*" began Song. His gaze drifted out of focus, then snapped back. "*Yes. In a way, you are a dex. Well, halfway. You're my tenth child.*"

A whisper of cold air shivered its way up Moon's spine. "I'm a tenth child."

"*You are.*"

"Can *I* be a tribute?"

Song turned the question around again. "*Do you like that idea?*"

"Yes!" Moon's tail was practically spinning. "Will they let me be your tribute?"

"*I'll speak with Brook. And our Shinoo, of course. They'll know what can be done.*"

8

HIGHWIND SONG CIRCLE

Moon was around wolves all day, every day, so he'd sort of expected more of the same at the Highwind Song Circle. Wasn't that only natural, since their hosts were wolves? But the people thronging the gathering grounds came from dozens of different clans.

Moon hugged Marnoo close, rubbing his chin against the fuzz atop her head as he peered around, then way, way, *way* up at the ring of sentinel pines. "I didn't know trees could be this tall," he whispered.

Da glanced down with a smile. "There's nothing like this in Ambervelte territory."

"After a few days, I miss a clear view of the sky," remarked Song.

"How long will we be here?" They'd left in such a rush, it hadn't occurred to Moon to ask.

"Three weeks. Four if the dexes make plans."

"Which they always *do,"* said Song in teasing tones.

"This way to our allotment." Da strode off like he'd been here a thousand times. Maybe he had. He pointed out lanterns hung among the trees. "Learn the crests, and be courteous of any boundaries the other clans have set. Some are shyer than others, but most everyone who attends is here to be friendly."

People were dressed in festival finery. By far, the most prominent were Highwind colors—white upon midnight blue. But there were red-cloaked reindeer and squirrels in green tunics. Moon spotted the honey-gold of a bear clan. The brilliant blue of a crow clan. And a crowd of songbirds wearing sashes in every color of the rainbow.

Moon's nose was working fast, there was so much to take in.

A group of children trotted by, some from every clan.

"Let's get settled in the tents," said Da. "Then you can join in on their games."

That sounded fun. "Do you have friends from other clans?"

"Many friends," replied Da. "Dexes are called on to patrol during Song Circles and festivals, so I have lots of opportunities. You'll see how it is once you start your training."

"I can train? As a dex?"

"Shinoo agrees. You have the makings of a protector. We'll consider you set apart and begin your training after we return home."

Moon whispered his news into Marnoo's silky ear. "Hear that, cub of my heart? Your Moon is a dex."

9

CONFLUENCE

Moon wasn't so sure he liked the Song Circle. Strangers didn't know him, so they assumed he was just a whelp with enough baby fuzz to count as cute. He couldn't really blame them. His own parents weren't sure how being Kith-kin had meddled with how he was aging. Several Ambervelte Kith who'd been born *after* Moon that were already flirting with prospective mates.

Da's best guess was that Moon was maturing physically like one of the Kindred instead of as a Kith. However, he had a Kith's clarity and emotional maturity. Moon had reached his attainment because his parents acknowledged him as an adult, but he needed to be patient. In a century or two, his body would catch up.

Moon had cause to be glad. He'd probably be longer-lived than Kith.

But here and now? He was tired of being treated like a child.

And there were whispers. First, people noticed that Moon was different. Then they'd noticed that he had two fathers, and the explanations bandied about weren't always kind.

Moon began to hang back, to linger in truest form, and to mingle with the Kith.

"You're the one, aren't you?"

The sudden question sent Moon's tail tucking. He whirled to face a beautiful person with long white hair and splendid blue eyes, who was draped in cloth that shimmered with hidden rainbows.

"You can't hide the truth. Not when the lyrics of lorefolk are tattling on you." And crouching down, he said, "Speaking form, please."

Moon didn't want to show himself, but he shifted anyhow. Of course he would. But he felt his cheeks begin to burn.

Radiating delight, the stranger said, "Kith-kin! Not many of *you* flitting about. It's a pleasure. I'm known as Opal the Sage. Tell me your name."

"Moon-kin Ambervelte."

"Have you been hearing things, Moon-kin Ambervelte?" Opal casually lifted a finger to indicate the sky.

There was a melody in the air, almost like wolfsong. But it thrummed so much deeper than the voices of the packs, and there were words. As he strained his ears to catch their meaning, the voice split several ways, soaring in chorus. Eight. Twelve. Twenty. His gaze lifted to the lights that were dancing just out of sight beyond the treetops.

"Do *you* hear that?" whispered Moon.

"We are surrounded by sounds. Can you be more specific?"

Moon pointed up. "Someone is singing."

"Those are the stars, dear boy. The stars are singing. For you ...?"

He slowly shook his head, but he wasn't quite sure. "I've been hearing them since Marnoo was born. I think they're singing for her."

"And who is Marnoo?"

"My ... umm. She's mine. I'm fostering my baby sister."

"What an idea! You are hardly more than a baby yourself."

He stood straighter. "I've reached my attainment."

"Many felicitations on your advancement," Opal smoothly returned. "You know, wolves are not often favored by stars. They have neatly knotted their lives to the Moon. Your namesake, I suppose. Lovely lady."

It almost sounded like Opal knew the Moon personally.

His ears pricked. Was that his name he'd heard?

"So you *can* hear them. Not everyone does. I wonder if it is because you are Kith-kin. Your wilder instincts are working in your favor." Opal gazed upward. "My advice to you, Moon-kin Ambervelte, is to listen well. Few ever guess at the Maker's purposes, and fewer still can guess correctly. But this you should mark, and so let it move you. You are not hearing stars for no reason, even if that reason is as small as it is simple."

They were important-sounding words, but Moon couldn't figure out if they meant anything. But ... he didn't mind listening to Opal. The sound of his voice made Moon hope he'd say something else. So he asked, "I should listen?"

"Listen well. And with pleasure." He smiled and said, "Enjoy it. I always have."

So Moon stood with face upturned, listening.

He was still there when Song found him.

A nip to his ear stirred Moon.

"Here you are. Shinoo is asking for you. Didn't her voice reach you?"

Moon could remember Opal telling him to listen to the stars. Their voices were the only ones he'd been listening to, even though he was having a hard time sorting out what their songs meant.

Song was drawing long breaths. *"What were you doing out here with the dragon bard?"*

"I was listening." Moon had done his very best. "He told me to listen to the stars."

With a grumbling huff, his sire nudged him toward their encampment. *"Opal can be so irresponsible. I'll have Brook speak with him about this. For now, come in out of the cold. Marnoo will be wanting her Moon."*

"Is Opal … bad?"

"No. He has our pack's trust. Everyone's really. But with dragons, it can be … well, I'll let Brook explain it, dex to dex."

"Are they tricksters?" Moon checked. His mother had warned him about their mischief.

Instead of answering, Song paused and craned his neck skyward. *"Did you hear that?"*

If he meant the stars, then yes. Hadn't he said that he was listening? But others were calling out, and soon people from every clan were peering up through the trees or simply taking flight, wanting a better view.

Because ribbons of shining color slowly rippled through the sky.

Moon didn't realize he was rising toward them until Song caught the hem of his tunic, holding him back. The shock of it put the notion of stars from Moon's mind.

"Thought so," his sire grumbled, though he sounded amused. *"No flying off until Brook establishes your boundaries."*

Focus sharpening, Moon whispered, "I can fly?"

Song blandly revealed, *"Your da didn't want to bring it up until it came up naturally."*

Moon's feet reconnected with the snowy ground, but excitement made him so buoyant, he bounced back up again.

"Boundaries first," Song chided.

"Sorry," he mumbled, finding better footing. But his heart soared with every step toward their den.

10

WHISPERS

The next few days found Moon with a lot of time—and one increasingly wriggly cub—on his hands. Song had been right about dexes and their obligations. To prepare, Da had helped Shinoo to fill bottles with milk, enough that the cubs could get along without her until dawn.

"If Marnoo cries for more, see if any of our neighbors can make room for her alongside a litter."

Moon asked, "Are there other wolf cubs here?"

"*Any* mother among the clans would show kindness to Marnoo." Da suggested, "Try among the bears or the mountain lions. We've helped each other in years past."

So Moon carried Marnoo toward the circle, half-listening for stars, but also searching for any milk scents, just in case.

A voice tugged at his ears, and he soon

found his way to one of the sentinel pines, where a ring of people listened to Opal the Sage telling a story about someone called Fandriel. Moon laughed along with everyone else, because the story was funny. But people were taking notice again. And there were whispers among the children.

"What's wrong with him?"

"Can't he do it right?"

"Did you see his ears?"

Moon didn't feel like explaining himself, even though Da had gently pointed out that curiosity was natural. So when Marnoo began to whine for milk, Moon was glad for the excuse to slip away.

He soothed her with a sop until she drifted off again, and he let his own eyes close. He was sifting through the many sounds when a deep rumble startled him into wariness. A black wolf sat a short distance away, his tail slowly swaying.

Only after Moon nodded a polite greeting did the wolf shift into speaking form.

"Peace, Kindred. My name is Doon-wen Nightspangle." And sitting in the snow before him, he quietly asked, "You are Kith-kin?"

"I'm Moon-kin Ambervelte."

With a solemn nod, he said, "Peace, Moon-kin. And who is this?"

"Marnoo is mine," he snapped. But better manners asserted themselves. "Marnoo-vel Ambervelte. Da gave her to me to foster."

His words were too few to really explain, but the adults talked just as much as the children. And Da's children had been welcomed into many packs. Maybe even this one's.

Doon-wen reached out, but he hesitated, brows lifting a little as he waited for permission to touch. Moon thought he wanted to pet Marnoo, who was so soft. But the wolf's big hand came to rest on his shoulder.

"Your parents must be overjoyed."

He said it so warmly, Moon's tail remembered how to wag.

"Which one is Kith?"

"Song. My sire is Kith."

"Ah. It is the other way around in my den. My bondmate is Kith."

"Are … are you a dex?"

"No."

Moon blushed and mumbled, "My sire, Song ... he loves our Shinoo."

"That is the way of things with bondmates," Doon-wen agreed easily.

"Your children are Kith?" he dared to ask.

"They are."

"Any Kith-kin?"

"Not as yet. Someday, if the Maker is generous."

Moon was fascinated. "You want a Kith-kin child?"

Doon-wen put up a hand. "I am not dissatisfied with any of my sons or daughters, but True—my bondmate—wants such a treasure for me."

"I don't know any other Kith-kin."

"No wonder, given how rarely one makes an appearance." His gaze was heavy. "I hope you have been properly welcomed."

Moon wasn't sure he should complain. "The others ... stare."

"Mmm. If you are looking for playmates, look for the Nightspangle lantern. And if Marnoo is in need while Shinoo-dex's duties keep her apart, one of my daughters has milk.

Show yourself to a Kith named Task. She is as gentle as she is generous."

"Th-thank you!" he managed.

Doon-wen gave his shoulder a light squeeze, then excused himself, his tail flagging as he strolled away.

Moon buried his nose in Marnoo's fur, then whispered, "He said … *overjoyed*. About my being Kith-kin." It was nice to be thought of as a treasure instead of an oddity.

11

STARRY ONE

A week passed, then another, and every day was both the same and different. The things Marnoo needed never changed, so Moon ranged between their shelter and the Nightspangle one, where Task encouraged her cubs to be gentle with the star-white cub who came to visit.

While she suckled, Moon played with Task's trio of children, who were a few weeks older than Marnoo and full of energy. He tussled with them while in truest form, then amazed them by shifting into speaking form to reclaim his sister.

"Aren't you Kith?"

"I was born Kith, same as you."

"Can I do that, Mam?"

"No, love. We're the strength of the Night-spangle pack, but we can't take speaking form like your grandsire or like Moon-kin. Aren't

Kith-kin amazing?"

"He is! Oh, you are!"

"Come again?" they pleaded each time. *"Play with us again?"*

"Next time Marnoo is hungry and her bottle is empty," he promised.

Somehow, these cubs' questions didn't bother him the way those of other children had. Was it only because they were so little? Or was he getting more used to the questions, so he didn't mind them as much? It didn't hurt that they thought him amazing. Maybe that was Doon-wen's influence?

Moon cut through a stand of young conifers, working his way around behind the boundaries of other allotments. A sound tugged at his attention, and he pricked his ears, searching for its repetition. Was that ... his name?

Yes, someone was calling for him.

He should answer, but he couldn't figure out where the voice was coming from. It didn't ring in his ears, but it also didn't feel like a wolf.

"I'm here," he offered uncertainly. And a

little louder, "Here I am."

"This way, child of packs. I am not far from where you are. Follow my light and find me."

Suddenly, there was a glow up among the branches of an enormous old oak. Moon took a step toward it, then another.

"Yes. I am here," the voice came again.

Moon glanced around, but nobody else seemed to be nearby or noticing. But he was sure, sure, *sure* that he should chase this light. So he picked up his paws and trotted, then disobeyed his beloved Song by lifting off the ground, rising toward that beckoning glow.

"Slowly, wolfling. Choose a sturdy branch, and I will meet you there."

He quickly diverted to a broad limb and sank to his knees upon it, hugging Marnoo close and murmuring in her ear. Her eyes blinked open, and their coppery sheen reflected the shape of the person descending.

"Moon-kin Ambervelte."

The voice rang in his thoughts, as clear and piercing as a howl, full of authority, but somehow not scary. Moon had never heard of imps being dangerous. He had imps in his ancestry. His tail stirred against rough bark, and he dared to lift his gaze. "That's me. I'm Moon. Are ... are you a star?"

"This night, I am a messenger."

He tipped his head to one side, then the other. "That's probably fine. As long as you don't try to take Marnoo."

The star actually looked surprised. *"I would not do that."*

"In stories, wolves like to carry moon maidens into their dens. Doesn't that mean that a moonbeam or a star could carry a Widelander into the sky if they wanted?" With that thought, he found he could bare his teeth a little, to show this star that he would defend his sister if necessary.

"Brave boy, let me begin in a better place." And taking a very wolvish posture that promised peace, the star said, *"I am Soriel, and I speak for the One who made all things."*

Was that ... the Maker? Moon blushed. Was he being rude to the Maker?

"You are needed."

He countered, "Marnoo needs me."

"Someone else." The star's posture wilted

into something more pleading. *"Will you listen?"*

He bit his lip and nodded.

Soriel pointed. *"Walk that way. Bring your sister, and walk until you can walk no further, and then wait there."*

"Am I allowed to ask why?" He fidgeted. "What will I be waiting for?"

"Someone who needs you will find you where you are. Be in that place. Be there for him."

He looked off in the direction that Soriel had pointed. "That way?" he asked doubtfully.

But instead of an answer, the light winked out, and Moon was alone with Marnoo ... and with a choice to make.

12

FOUNDLINGS

Moon hesitated at the base of the tree. His starry messenger had said to go one way, but there was Marnoo to consider. If he was going to walk as far as he could one way—which would carry them a *long* way— he shouldn't go without a fresh bottle of milk. So he trotted toward the Ambervelte shelter.

Song was there, watching over the sleep of a couple of denmates who'd needed to go deep. *"Welcome back."*

"I have to go again." Moon checked for milk and found a still-warm bottle.

"You could leave Marnoo," Song offered.

"I need her with me." He wasn't sure how much else he should say. Perhaps his tucked tail spoke for him, because his sire radiated concern.

"I'll call Brook back. One of us can go with you ...?"

"I have to go alone, I think."

Song's ears pricked, and he looked up, as if he could see past the roof of their shelter. Was he hearing stars, too? Maybe so, because when his gaze found Moon's again, all he said was, *"Nose to the trail. I'll be here when you return."*

So Moon cradled Marnoo close, found his bearing and began to walk.

And walk.

And walk.

They were far from the lanterns and songs when Marnoo needed a break. Moon cared for her, then shifted in order to curl around her, rumbling comfort and whispering endearments that only she could hear.

His ears pricked at the first sound of footfalls.

He held still, wary of strangers, especially one that might get in the way of his mission. Maybe they were a dex on patrol, and they'd try to send Moon back. What if they thought Moon was too young to be so far? Or worse, what if they tried to take Marnoo away?

It *was* a wolf. A male with downcast eyes.

Was he tracking them?

Marnoo whimpered, and Moon snapped, *"I won't let you take her! She's mine!"*

He faltered, and his face came up. Silver eyes widened, and he ventured, "What are you doing way out here?"

And despite Moon's posturing, the big stranger—a Highwind by his coloring and by the festival colors of his tunic—took Marnoo and made room for her under the layers of his clothes, holding her close with one big hand.

He wanted to bring her back, but that wasn't what the star had said.

Needing hands, Moon shifted into speaking form, but all his snarling was met by a mild gaze and a melancholy smile. "Peace, whelp. Would you have me ignore her needs?"

Chastised, Moon scooted closer. *"I'm here,"* he soothed. *"Your Moon is here."*

And in her little baby voice, Marnoo answered, *"Moon, Moon, Moooooon."*

He relaxed a little, smiled a little, and endured the usual questions.

The Highwind wolf's brows rose, but he accepted Moon's revelations without a trace of criticism. "This is a pleasure!"

So they talked for a while, and Loor-ket Highwind—for that was his name—called Moon "good lad," and he sounded like he didn't want to go back to the Song Circle any more than Moon did.

"A little longer?" Moon begged. "I came prepared."

So they fed Marnoo together, and she was so cute, grumbling and lapping up the milk that spilled into Loor's palm. And somehow, he didn't make Moon feel like a child when he coaxed him onto his lap so they could shelter Marnoo together. Loor was interesting—sort of serious and sort of quiet—and he seemed as glad as Moon to have someone to talk to.

Hoping to hold him there even longer, Moon asked for a story.

Loor obliged.

"There once was a set of twins. Two brothers who were so alike, even the Moon couldn't tell them apart. So their mother knotted white stones around the wrist of one and smooth bones around the wrist of the other. One embraced the life of a dex, becoming the favorite of every Kith and being respected by the Kindred. The other was his grumpy younger twin, whose only weapon was a needle and whose only friend was a Kith-kin."

He joked about learning to sew because his mother mistook him for a daughter, but Moon could tell that he was proud of his skills. Lightly touching the embroidery that made Loor's festival tunic beautiful, he dared to ask, *"Do they tease you?"*

Sadness dulled silver eyes. "Worse. They never noticed."

Moon leaned into Loor's strength and took his words to heart. He liked to think about having a place and learning your purpose.

One detail might have slipped past, except Moon was good at picking up scents.

With a smile, he murmured, "Loor?"

"Hmm?"

"Am I really your only friend?"

"Without you and Marnoo, I'd be wretchedly alone." Loor kissed his forehead. "I'm glad our paths crossed, Moon-kin. You are my friend for life."

13

TELL ME A STORY

Moon approved of questions.

On principle.

He'd asked Song and Da *so* many questions when he was a cub. All kinds of questions about all kinds of things. And they'd always encouraged his curiosity. So he, in his turn, was definitely willing to answer all of five-year-old Marnoo's questions. He just wished they weren't always the *same* question. Or a variation on her favorite theme.

"Will you tell me Loor-ket's story?" she begged sweetly. *"Tell me about your friend."*

"I've told you a hundred times. Maybe even a thousand."

She rolled onto her back and waved her paws in the air. *"Tell it again?"*

Moon grumbled, "There are other wolves in the world. Good ones. Kind ones."

"Not as good as Loor. Not kinder." She

stubbornly insisted, *"He's my favorite."*

And even though he sort of thought that *he* should've been Marnoo's favorite, just like always, Moon gave in.

"When I was smaller than I am now, barely big enough to lift you, since you were quite an armful, even if you *were* the runt of your litter ...."

"That's not part of the story!"

"It is," he countered. "Because I had to carry you through deep snow, which was up to my hips in some places."

"You're skipping ahead!" Marnoo complained. *"Tell why you had to push through snowbanks."*

Because she knew the story as well as he did. So well, she probably could have sung it forward, then backward. So he chose a place closer to the beginning.

"It was my first Song Circle, and even though you and Hynoo and Jinyoo were so tiny to be traveling far from home, we carried you north."

"For you."

"Partly, yes. Da and Mam and Song wanted to present me to the packs and give my name its extra flourish."

"*Because you're Kith-kin.*"

"I am."

"*Did the packs welcome you?*"

She asked every time, and his answer was still changing. Because he was more comfortable with his differences now. And because meeting a star had a way of dimming other memories. And because other Kith-kin had heard of him and had come to meet him, many directed to his den by Doon-wen Nightspangle.

"I was welcomed with song." He tugged her ear. "And then I presented you to the packs, singing your name."

"*Because you chose it!*"

"Because I chose it."

"*Did Loor-ket welcome you?*"

"*Now* who's skipping ahead."

She giggled and butted at his hand, expectant.

"I'd noticed the stars before. I'd been hearing songs since before you were born. Just snatches of lyrics, but they tickled my ears and made me wonder. A dragon bard told me to listen, so even after we returned to our home here, I would go out at night."

"To the hill with the silver trees you planted."

"That's the place."

"My favorite place."

"I wanted to make us a little song circle of our own. A place we could share and fill with good memories."

"Tell about the star now," she ordered. *"The star in the treetops."*

"A star came down, and he told me his name. Da says that he's an important messenger from the Maker. People call him Soriel of the Dawning."

"Was he beautiful?"

"Yes. And so bright, I almost couldn't look at him."

"Because he was shining. Because he's a star."

"He is."

"And he spoke."

"He said I should take you and walk away."

"That's all?"

"That's all."

"And you didn't know why or what for or who?"

"Not anything."

"But you went."

"That is the essence of faith."

Marnoo's wriggled closer. *"Are you glad you did?"*

"I wonder."

"You're smiling."

"Am I?"

"Your tail is wagging."

"Is it?"

"Tell more!" she demanded.

Because his girl always wanted to know more. She never got enough of the story, and she was especially fascinated by Loor-ket Highwind. Meeting him was an event that bound them together. A story they traded back and forth. A memory full of starlight and miracles and song. It was theirs and theirs alone. Until the day Terloo-soh Ambervelte returned after the bonding journey she'd taken with her new mate. There was a tumult over their arrival, and Moon came running.

He found Marnoo dancing at their feet, yipping and chanting, *"Loor! Loor! Loor!"*

"Loor-ket?" whispered Moon, shocked by his sudden appearance.

But the clansman's silver-eyed gaze only held confusion.

Moon tried to pull Marnoo away, to get her to settle down. He was remembering parts of the story that he didn't always tell. Loor-ket had spoken about two brothers who were so much alike, their own mother had trouble telling them apart.

He searched for—and found—a simple bracelet at his wrist. One with white bones.

Marnoo kept wriggling, trying to get at the one with a kindred scent Moon hadn't even realized she remembered. The newcomer crouched, offering his hands to Marnoo, who nosed and licked and crooned, *"Same, same, same!"*

Moon gruffly said, "Hush, Marnoo. This isn't Loor-ket."

The wolf's eyes widened, and he hastily glanced around. "Is Loor-ket here?"

"Are you his twin?" asked Moon.

All of the sudden, a little girl was pulling on this twin's vest, then grabbing a handful of hair in order to pull him in range for the kisses she pressed to his jaw. Her tail twirled and her voice sweetly continued her litany. "Same, same, same. I know you! Mine, mine, Loor is mine!"

Moon stood stunned. Marnoo had made her first shift into speaking form, and her first words weren't for Moon. They were for this stranger. Or … for Loor-ket.

He shed his own vest to cover her. Blushing badly over her manners, Moon said, "No, Marnoo. It's not him. Loor had a twin. Remember the story? A twin brother."

"Hello, little one," said the wolf, whose gentle voice almost matched Moon's memories. "I'm not the Loor you so clearly love. My name is Beloor-dex. I'm his twin."

"Moon-kin?" ventured Terloo, who'd brought this dex into the Ambervelte pack. "You met Loor-ket?"

Tears shining in silver eyes, Beloor asked, "Do you know where my brother went?"

14

HANDFUL

Moon took slow, patient breaths as he considered possibilities. Marnoo wasn't where she was supposed to be, but that didn't mean she was in any kind of danger. Not here, in the heart of their pack's territory. Assuming she *was* here. Maybe he should check their circle of birches? She still visited it sometimes.

Grasses rippled in gusting wind, and the shushing sound that usually soothed him felt like chiding. "I know, I know," he murmured. "I'm disappointed in me, too."

Maybe it was because of Da's ancestry, but the winds were always so nosy about Marnoo. Right now, they seemed to sigh over some new trouble he hadn't managed to prevent. It was a good thing that Moon had hands, because Marnoo was a handful.

She wasn't a helpless cub anymore, but

she wasn't past minding. Marnoo was his responsibility, but she wasn't easily contained. As flighty as her da, and as headstrong as their mam.

He mentally turned to the ones who always heard him out. *"I lost Marnoo."*

"Again?" His mother's voice held no trace of worry, only amusement.

"Are we not trackers?" asked Song. He was definitely laughing.

Moon grumbled, *"I know how to track, but I taught her, so she also knows how to obscure a trail. Her most recent steps crisscross all her favorite places, but she probably skimmed off."*

Ever since Marnoo had learned to shift into speaking form, touching the ground was completely optional. She could flit about like the breezes that chased her.

"She doesn't usually go far," offered Da.

"If she took the time to lay false trails, then she is trying to delay you," said Shinoo.

Song asked, *"Is there anywhere you recently told her not to go?"*

Moon groaned.

His baby sister was usually so obedient.

It had been months since he'd put his foot down, trying to give Beloor and Terloo some much needed privacy as they readied their den for their first child. And while Marnoo was early in her adolescence, she was getting too old to be frisking around another she-wolf's bonded.

"I know where she's gone."

"Is it any wonder?" asked Da, who'd probably known all along.

Really, Moon should have realized sooner.

Shinoo's voice came again. *"Do not be too harsh with her, Moon-kin. She is only following her heart."*

Moon thanked them and ran toward the one place Marnoo wasn't supposed to be.

Terloo met him at the entrance to the shelter she shared with her bondmate. Her smile was sympathetic, and her tail swayed calmly. "It's all right, Moon-kin. We've missed her visits."

He drooped. "I'm sorry for the intrusion. Again."

"Bel loves any excuse to talk about his twin."

"But every day? Marnoo has to be trespassing upon your patience."

"What's the harm? She is bright and funny, and it's not Beloor who has her heart." Terloo bluntly added, "Loor-ket is her choice."

"An impossible choice. He's gone."

"Paths that have crossed once can cross again." Terloo slipped an arm around his shoulders and steered him toward the sound of voices within. "Come inside. We've missed you, too, Moon-kin."

Inside, Marnoo was hiding behind Beloor, looking woebegone. "Don't be mad, Moon! A star was singing so sweetly, and before I knew it, I was here."

Moon sat and held out his arms.

His sister tumbled into them and clung, and he let all his worries and frustrations melt away. Looking over her head at Beloor, he spoke the truth. "You're too kind."

"I would hardly turn her away. The things she wants are simple and easy to share."

Marnoo said, "He tells me stories about Loor."

"You can't possibly remember him."

"I do, too!" And rearranging herself so that she sat upon Moon's lap, she said, "Tell another story, please."

Moon probably should have protested, but if he was honest, he wanted to hear a story as well.

Beloor smiled knowingly and said, "I'll tell you both."

15

STARRY HOPES

Usually, Moon had to go to Beloor's door in order to find his sister, so he was surprised when, on a winter's day, for the first time ever, Beloor came to his. "Peace, friend."

"Be welcome," Moon returned, easing quickly into a receptive posture. "Do you or one of yours have need of me?"

"Not exactly. Not in the way you mean. We're fine. That … isn't it."

So there *was* something. And Beloor seemed almost flustered. His faint smile was a true thing, but his emotions were in disarray. Moon was having trouble tracking their source … let alone what they meant. Beloor had been his friend for a long time. As fellow dexes, they'd trained together with each sunrise, and Bel's bonded counted Marnoo as a sister. So deep was their trust that several of Terloo's cubs had been born into Marnoo's hands.

Yet Beloor's tail hung limp.

Moon quietly invited, "Tell me."

"My time as a dex spans so many centuries. I've learned ancient secrets, and I've seen many miracles. But never once did I think I would be saying these words to you." Beloor cleared his throat, then declared, "A star came down."

All the fur on Moon's body stood up.

With careful deliberation, Beloor brought out a cloth-wrapped bundle. "This is for Marnoo."

Moon slowly unwrapped a lovely hand-carved comb. The gift was … confusing. Marnoo had been variously ignoring, rebuffing, and laughing off the attentions of hopeful males for a very long time. Anyone with ears knew the reason. Marnoo had been declaring her choice almost since she could speak.

"Why would you give Marnoo a courting comb?"

Beloor slowly shook his head. "It is not for her. Well, it *is*. But not from my hand. That is a gift for my brother. My twin. Give that to Loor-ket."

"How am I to do that? Nobody knows where he is. We've asked every pack at every Song Circle, and no one took in a Highwind wolf."

"Go east," said Beloor. "Watch for his star. It will be shining over a place unlike any other."

"What does that mean?"

"Soriel did not explain." Beloor softly added, "And I did not have the wits to ask, since I was trembling so badly."

"A star in the east." Moon carefully rewrapped the comb. "Am I to bring him home?"

"After so long?" Beloor sounded skeptical.

Moon nodded, then shook his head. "Will you look after Marnoo while I'm away?"

With a soft laugh, he countered, "You have to know that you won't go alone. Do your part, Moon. Bring Marnoo home."

16

FOLLOW

I wanted to go sooner," Marnoo admitted, gazing up into the starfield above. "To run away. To go rogue."

Moon stole a peek at her profile. "I can only assume you didn't because someone raised you better than that."

She grinned. "Taking the credit, are you?"

"I'll settle for blame. If you'd gone the way Loor did, without a word, it would have broken my heart."

"I know."

"Why did you stay?"

"Because the stars told me to wait."

That was a sobering thought. Moon reached for the hand that wouldn't be his to hold for much longer. "That must have been difficult."

Marnoo sighed. "Every day was a struggle. No, I'm sure it was every minute. But I knew that if I didn't listen, I'd lose him. So I endured it."

Moon whispered, "I let you suffer …?"

"Don't be silly." She turned to fully face him and tugged one of his drooping ears upright. "You're the only Moon I ever needed."

That was nice to hear. He'd cherish the knowledge after … well, *after*.

He wryly said, "We're a couple of star-addled wolves. We don't even know where to go." The winds stirred fitfully.

"East," she said, tucking white hair behind the dainty point of one ear.

"Well, yes. East. But a direction isn't a trail, and I'm more comfortable … umm … Marnoo?"

She'd gasped. And then grabbed his ear, using it to turn his head. "There. Do you see it? Just there."

He searched the sky and found a dancing twinkle of light. "Yes," he whispered back, suddenly tense. "Is that star … dancing?"

Marnoo stared fixedly, as if she was afraid that it would be gone if she blinked. "Ohhh," she breathed. "Oh, Moon. They're beckoning. That's our guide."

Moon thought so, too. "Want to run?"

"I want to *fly*." But Marnoo didn't move. Copper eyes wide, she whispered, "What if he refuses?"

With a snort, Moon tugged her along by hand, just as he'd done many, many, many times before. "Loor-ket is my friend. My friend for life. He couldn't possibly be a fool."

17

FINALLY

I'm your go-between. Let me speak to him first. I want to make sure that he's worthy of the one I've always treasured."

"The cub of your heart?" she lightly teased.

"You always will be," he promised. "I'm prepared to let you go to him, but not unless he remembers. If he's forgotten us, I'll defy the stars and even the One who made them."

Marnoo flung her arms around him. "You used to say I couldn't remember."

"I did say that sometimes. I was young and foolish. Today, I'll make amends. And make sure you've found a good den."

"The best of dens." She stepped back and gave him a little push.

So Marnoo held back while Moon shifted into truest form and sniffed along a boundary line that was enforced by wards. He caught a whiff of squirrel and knew better than to trust his eyes. But more prevalent by far was the scent of the kinds of livestock that humans tended … and a wolf-scent.

The stars were singing again, and he pricked his ears.

His voice was too small for the expanse, nothing like the chorusing of stars. Even so, Moon didn't shout or even sing out. In the quietness of his soul, he ventured, *"Soriel?"*

And just like before, a voice brushed his mind, giving his words back. *"I am here."*

"What do I do?"

"Call for him," replied the angel. *"Call, and he will answer."*

So Moon threw back his head and sang the name of his friend, watching his breath puff up and away, toward the stars that had been singing out of reach for all his years. He sang out the name of Loor-ket, to let him know that he wasn't forgotten.

18

THERE IS A WOLF

A clear note shrilled through the moonless night. A whistle? A summons!

Moon leapt in the direction, running on all fours, barging through thickets in the direction of the call. He spied Loor-ket standing with arms folded across his chest, his expression grim. Not the most welcoming aspect, but … *finally*!

Shifting on the fly, Moon tumbled into a two-legged sprint and spotted the moment when his friend recognized him. Confusion vanished, and he spread his arms wide in welcome. They collided, and Loor swung him around.

Moon wrapped his arms around his friend's neck and laughed. Finding his voice, his relief and happiness overflowed. "Found you, found you, found you!"

Gathering him into a snug embrace, Loor

exclaimed, "Moon-kin! Why are you here?"

"To find you." He needed to do this right. Easing out of Loor's arms, Moon stood tall and declared, "I had to keep my promise."

Strange. Moon had spent so many years marveling over how much Beloor-dex looked like Loor-ket. But now, it was the other way around, because Beloor's was the face he knew better. While Loor-ket did greatly resemble his brother, many differences had taken hold during their centuries apart.

Quirks of expression … and fashion.

Less beads, more embroidery.

The boots were baffling.

As was Loor's lack of a tail.

But Moon would have known him anywhere. And best, best, best of all, Loor-ket remembered him. It was a good start.

Loor grunted and wrapped his arms around Moon again, giving pricked ears an affectionate scratch. "Why would you need a loner like me?"

"I promised Marnoo."

He considered that before shaking his head. "How is your fosterling?"

"She's strong, and her will is stronger." This was it. He needed to do his part. Pushing back again, searching his friend's face, he took a formal tone. "I am Marnoo-vel Ambervelte's go-between. She will have you and no other."

Loor couldn't have looked more bewildered. Hands framing the size of the runt he'd met, he asked, "Your half-sister?"

Holding his hand up to indicate her current height, he cheerfully said, "My half-sister."

He rubbed at a forehead that was marked by a gleaming copper star, just the color of Ambervelte eyes. "I met you once and briefly. We shared stories in a snowbank until you fell asleep, and I carried you to your people. That's all."

"You made a lasting impression."

"That was never my intent."

"Yet to Marnoo, you are the scent of stars, the voice of an angel, and the hope of all her somedays." Moon pushed closer, plying Loor with questions, trying to decide if his friend's faltering explanations were meant for excuses.

And then a new voice called into that inner

place where anyone from the wolf clans could speak their minds. No, not just wolves. Because Loor was a dog now. As was the silver-eyed Kith who stepped into the open.

"I will speak for my father," said a big dog with fur the same color as Loor-ket's hair. *"He is Glint Starmark, First of Dogs, Friend of Beacons, Founder of Wardenclave."*

19

MOON'S BLESSING

Loor-ket—no, his name was *Glint* now—gestured between them. "This is my eldest son Path. I have become a Kith-sire."

Moon's tail swung higher at this news. Song and Da and their Shinoo walked the same path. Theirs was a different sort of den, but not *so* different. And it quickly became clear that Path was another person who'd been listening to stars.

Moon sent word to Marnoo. *"We were foretold."*

Her answering laughter was part relief, part triumph. Living by faith wasn't as simple as it sounded. Moon was increasingly certain that they were where they needed to be. Marnoo had reached the place she belonged. But ... Glint needed to agree. It was time for Moon to play go-between.

He said, "If I am the moon, then Marnoo is its radiance."

Beloor's gift! In all the excitement, Moon had nearly forgotten. It should come first.

Glint gasped and took the bundle of copper cloth, his nostrils quivering.

"A betrothal gift. Prepared for Marnoo-vel by Beloor-dex Ambervelte with every blessing … and a promise." As Glint unwrapped the courting comb, Moon quietly added, "If you wish it, he will come to stand by your side and bear witness to your bonding."

Voice rough with emotion, Glint asked, "Bel would come here?"

Then Marnoo stepped into the open in truest form.

Glint was so still, his expression utterly rapt. Moon thought it a good sign.

When she took speaking form, Glint grew so flustered, Moon could see why Bel had always called his brother shy, gruff, and awkward with others. But Glint stood his ground while Marnoo looked him over. Made up her mind. Paid him compliments.

His posture betrayed nothing, and he had no tail to signal his mood. So Moon watched closely, needing to be sure, still ready to intervene.

But Marnoo's mind had been made up for centuries. She asked, "Glint Starmark, First of Dogs, Friend of Beacons, Founder of Wardenclave, has my journey been worthwhile? Or will you send me into solitude?"

Stars were singing again.

Glint's eased into a receptive posture.

Marnoo kissed him.

All was going well until Glint's claim took a shape that Moon couldn't have anticipated. A name. He'd be giving her a new name. Which meant that Moon's first gift would be cast aside and forgotten. She'd no longer be Marnoo-vel, his song.

A trifling thing.

Yet so dismaying.

Thankfully, Glint didn't notice. He only had eyes for Marnoo, and her smile held a saucy sort of challenge when she urged him to choose with care.

"Do not be sad. You can trust Da. He is good at names."

Moon's gaze jumped to Path, whose tail gave a tense little shiver. The barest of wags. Like he wasn't sure his input would be welcomed.

"I named her. She has a name because I chose it."

Silver eyes went soft with sympathy. *"I apologize. You can be sad. I think I would be sad."*

"Only a little sad," Moon confided. *"It makes me happy that they are happy."*

"Tell me?" suggested Path. *"I would like to know more about Da's bondmate. Tell me the story of her name?"*

How many times had Marnoo begged for stories? Moon knew better than anyone that stories could be bridges. That they could connect lives. And the story Path wanted to learn was one that would forever connect Marnoo and Moon.

Moon showed his palms to Path. *"I'm willing. I definitely will. But we should* trade stories."

Path's tail gave a tentative thump, but his attention swung toward his father, and his floppy ears pricked.

Glint's lips were pressed to Marnoo's

forehead, and when he drew back, a sparkle remained. A tiny star now marked his sister's brow, silver as Glint's wide eyes.

Bewilderment blossomed into wonderment, and his posture took on the kind of pride and possessiveness for which wolves were famous. And dogs, apparently. Glint kissed her softly and established their bond with a word that suited her perfectly. "Radiance."

There was no moon in tonight's sky, but he'd always been the only Moon that his cub needed. The blessing was his to bestow. But how were words supposed to capture the enormity of patient endurance and single-minded dedication that had spanned centuries?

Moon searched his store of close-kept treasures and found one that might suit. Flinging his arms around both of them, Moon pulled their heads to his shoulders, mussing their hair as he stared up into the winter-deep sky, where stars glinted and danced and sang and shared their radiance.

"Brave boy." He brushed a kiss to Glint's brow.

"My girl." He pressed his lips to the top of Radiance's head.

"I am overjoyed."

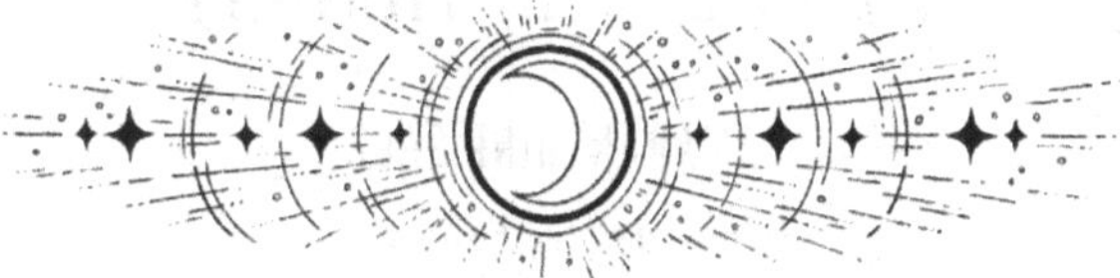

THE END

*Abundant thanks to all who lend their support
by reading, rating, and reviewing my stories,
wherever they may be found. ::twinkle::*

ALSO BY FORTHRIGHT

AMARANTHINE SAGA

Tsumiko and the Enslaved Fox

Kimiko and the Accidental Proposal

Tamiko and the Two Janitors

Mikoto and the Reaver Village

Fumiko and the Finicky Nestmate

Pimiko and the Uncharted Island

Rhomiko and the Confirmed Bachelor

SONGS OF THE AMARANTHINE

Marked by Stars

Followed by Thunder

Dragged through Hedgerows

Governed by Whimsy

Hemmed in Silver

Captured on Film

Bathed in Moonlight

Flattered by Flowers

Scribbled in Margins

Pressed into Service

AMARANTHINE INTERLUDES

Lord Mettlebright's Man

Suuzu and the Nine Nippets of Legend

Coop and the Elderbough Trackers

AMARANTHINE OUTTAKES

Once & Well

Sipping at Happiness

A Song for Moon

PATREON EXCLUSIVES

Bard & Barbarian

Kimiko and the Cycle of Moons

Boniface Smythe of the Stately House Smythes

IMMORTAL HOLMES

Folk-Spelled

Else-Moored